Inside

the

Gates of Doons

I0460489

MIRIKA MAYO
CORNELIUS

<u>Inside the Gates of Doons</u>

An Akirim Press publishing

Acknowledgements

All glory, honor, praise and total worship to God Almighty, Jesus Christ and Holy Spirit for my life, family, friends and this writing talent.

mirikacornelius.com

More Akirim Press Books

Books by Mirika Mayo Cornelius

Secret

Colored Lily: Poppa Took My Innocence

Paton

Ain't Quite What I Thought!

Ain't Quite What I Thought! 2

Inside the Gates of Doons

Sunny Sides of My Shade

Murders at Gabriel's Trails: The Complete 5 Part Series
plus bonus Sins of Bain

Books by Rod Cornelius

Diggin' Gold

The Trusted

Single Again

Ghetto Eyes

The Best Kept Secrets

Ugly

<u>Books by Cyan Deane</u>

Dead Man's Mayhem

Execution's Karma

Table of Contents

Inside the Gates

of

Doons

Prologue

"London Bridge is falling down," the children began to sing an old nursery rhyme passed down from generation to generation until one little girl suggests another idea.

"I don't want to play this boring game. We always play this, and we know what happens at the end."

"What?"

"Absolutely nothing," she retorted. "That's why I have a better idea. Let's play Duck Duck Goose, except this time, we change the ending. Whoever we tag gets locked in the closet in the dark until the next person gets caught."

The children were up in the spare room of the house while their parents were downstairs near the creek having a gathering. Everyone was dressed in their favorite clothes because it was a Labor Day weekend, therefore, favorite clothes consisted only of fun clothes. The children generally were ready to play in their shorts and T-shirts, but there was one little, seven years old boy who just moved into the neighborhood. He didn't play immediately, but only sat and watched everyone, not saying one word - not even hi. That changed when there was a knock at the door of the upstairs bedroom.

"I'll get it," a little boy said marching happily to the door, ready to start an awesome new game of Duck Duck Goose, but when he opened the door, he stood back to get a better look at the new boy who would be joining them for their Labor Day fun this year. Eventually, he spoke. "You coming to play, too?"

"Yes, Eric," responded the new boy.

"Whoa! He knows my name!" shouted the boy, totally surprised by the new boy knowing his name. He threw his hand up to his forehead while his mouth fell open. "How do you know my name already?"

Before the new child could answer, Shelby, the prissy and proper little girl who lived at the residence, got up to go greet him. She was the only one dressed in an off white dress that her mom insisted marked the start of the ban on the color white for the rest of the year due to it turning Fall.

"Hi!" She felt like a bigger girl now that she could introduce another person into her own little world. Shelby extended her hand. "What's your name?"

"Hi, Shelby." This was the only thing the boy said, never telling anyone his name. However, he did shake her hand, which he noticed made her feel very important, so important that she didn't even ask for his name again. Instead, she stuck her chest out and guided him inside by his hand. He simply followed.

The boy knew everyone's name. Besides Eric and Shelby, he had also watched intently as Brian and Veronica, the fraternal twins, consistently second guessed one another and argued over the smallest things, such as who was standing where and who was first. Therefore, when he was guided to where they were all sitting in a circle, he released Shelby's hand and asked the twins a question.

"Should I sit by you or," he asked the female twin before turning to her brother, "should I sit by you?"

This caused an eruption in the big playroom which the new boy stood and watched, never once sitting down because that was never his intention. The new boy loved figuring things out about people. He never really had any true friends because it was always puzzling to him why they cared so much or why it meant so much to everyone.

As the children argued, he glanced up at Eric who was laughing hysterically and spinning around in a circle, and while Shelby tried her best to set things back together in her small world of order, he pulled a pitch fork from the back of his trousers, the one that he took from the cookout while the parents were having fun. Then, he decided to play his own game.

"It's time to eat!" Shelby's mom ran upstairs after about thirty minutes, only to open the playroom door to four children leaning against the walls and the new little boy sitting sieza style with the bloody pitchfork on the floor. When he heard the door open, he stared back at her. She continuously screamed in horror, and he answered her screaming calmly.

"We were just playing a game."

Chapter One

"Levi, shut up. I'm so tired of you always trippin' about everything but yourself."

"You know you love me, Séa."

His short, dark-brown skinned girlfriend who not only aspires to be a print model, but looks like she would've been a runway model if she had more height, shoves him off of her shoulders and scoots over beside the restaurant's booth window, coming so close to it that the curls of her edgy, black hair cut press up against the side of the window.

"I love you, Levi, but you always make a mockery out of me," she frowns at her laid back, pecan brown boyfriend who sports a thin taped mustache and low mo-hawk. "That's not cool. You didn't have to tell anyone about how I sleep."

"It was a joke, babe," he explains, waving his long, basketball player sized arms out to the side. "Peanuts, tell her it was a joke, man," he says to his cousin who sits directly in front of him.

"Keep playing, Levi. I told you about calling me Peanuts. That's not my name, and Séa's right. You're always trying to clown people," he argues, shoving Levi's hand away from his forehead. "Get off me, man. Stop playing so much. Don't call me Peanuts again. My name is Pierre," he continues, adjusting his black eyewear into a level position after Levi knocked them sideways.

"More like Peter," Levi retorts.

"His name is Pierre, Levi. Cut it out! I want us to have a good day, geez," Maria chimes in feeling sorry for Pierre once again because since she's known them, Pierre has always been on the beat down end of a verbal match although he's very witty. It just always concludes with his older cousin Levi out sparring him through embarrassment. "Anyway, when is Roscoe coming? He's late," she asks, lightly bouncing up and down next to Pierre in the booth seat.

"No he's not. He's never late. As a matter of fact, he's out there in the parking lot," Levi responds, taunting Maria with a devilish tone. "Whispering something into some female's ear," he continues, licking his lips and staring at her embarrassment. "Probably gonna hook up with her later. You wanna go get him, Maria, before you miss your catch again?"

Maria places her head into her hands, and her hair falls over her face. "You're an ass, Levi."

"What did I do?" he asks, pretending to be unaware of the emotional poking he's doing at Maria's heart.

"Don't listen to him, girl. Roscoe isn't even out there. As a matter of fact," Séa continues, lifting her head up so that she can see beyond the cars in the parking lot, "he's just now pulling in, so ignore Levi. He's on one of those irritation kicks today." Séa continues to watch as Roscoe's car comes to a standstill before reconnecting her attention to the others at the table.

"He's just mean, that's all, Séa. Sometimes your man is a piece of work."

Levi leans in on Séa and gives her a kiss on the cheek. "Yeah," he agrees, "but I'm her piece of work."

Séa shoves him in his chest with her elbow. "Move! You're too much today, for real. Levi, chill…and wipe that off your shirt."

"Aww, Peanuts, give me your napkin, man," he says, looking down at his bleached white T-shirt that's now stained with greasy cheese from his cheese potatoes that sit in front of him. Instead of waiting on Pierre to pass the napkin, he snatches it from the side of Pierre's plate, causing Pierre to feel helpless against him once again.

They're all eating breakfast at a well known eatery for the very first time in weeks. College has let out, and now the five of them who have hung out together like a crew for about six years, are finally able to hang out again for the summer. Levi and Maria are the only ones who chose not to further their education, so they're always crossing paths in the neighborhood. Maria has a fairly nice job as assistant manager at a major hotel chain. As for Levi, he makes money however he can the legal way, and all of them are still partially supported by their parents monetarily, minus Roscoe.

Pierre and Séa are on break from their studies, Pierre having come back in town from out of state college where he majors in pre-med Biology and minors in something totally unrelated – Media Arts with concentration on photography. Séa remains in state at a university that's about forty-five minutes outside of the city, still able to date Levi.

When Levi finishes with the napkin, he tosses it over into Pierre's plate. "Thanks, Peanuts."

"What did I just tell you, Levi, dang, man. Stop calling me Peanuts! Take the napkin out of my food!" He throws it at his twenty-three year old's cousin's face, completely tired of being his prime target. "I'm going to the bathroom."

Levi laughs, "With your peanuts."

"Goodness, Levi, quit!" Séa shouts in defense of the nineteen year old and youngest of the bunch. It's only Séa who knows the reason behind Levi's picking on him. Most people think it's a solely a joke about the size of Pierre's manhood, however, it has nothing to do with that.

When he and Pierre were kids, Levi decided to catch his puppy's urine in a cup, and when Pierre wasn't looking, dumped it into his big bag of boiled peanuts that were bought from the corner store. They were hot and ready to eat, and as Levi sat down with his bag, he watched as Pierre grabbed his. Boiled peanuts were Pierre's favorite, so he wasted no time taking them apart and eating them, even sucking the outside shell. Thus, the name *Peanuts*. It wasn't until after Pierre was halfway finished the bag that Levi told him what he'd done, thinking it to be funny. Pierre never felt the same about boiled peanuts, but Levi is his constant reminder.

"Man, Séa, Peanuts is just too sensitive. How are you taking up for that man anyway when you're my lady, baby?"

"Maria's right. We want everyone to have a good summer get together, not just you. Be a team player is all I'm asking. It's not all about you," Séa states calmly, but irritated enough to roll her eyes and continue to press herself away from Levi who has already given up trying to get close to her after the elbow shove to the chest.

While Séa and Levi are arguing, Maria sits up straight, allowing her figure to prop up and fall correctly inside her tight clothing. Along with elevating her posture, she twists the jewelry on her neck so that it hangs properly while she flips her long, dark brown hair from her face, all this for the twenty-three year old, flawless brown skinned, built to last, young man coming through the restaurant's entrance – Roscoe. Of course, all the twitching and fiddling she's doing to make herself appear the top notch Puerto Rican catch alerts both Séa and Levi of the fact that her crush is coming through the restaurant doors behind them.

Levi turns around and stands to his feet to greet the friend that he fell out with a couple years ago, only in an effort to show Séa and the rest of the crew that he's the bigger man. "What's up, Roscoe, man!"

"What's up, Levi?" he responds, glancing at Séa quickly and then back at Levi. "I see you and Séa are still making it happen. How ya' doing, man?"

"I'm good. We're good," he stresses.

The two both slap hands and shake, but there are no other words exchanged, leaving them to the awkward, short silence until Pierre comes up from behind.

"Roscoe! You're still pumping that iron, I see. Don't have the muscle shirt on, but you're still bulging at the arms, man."

Roscoe turns around to greet the voice he knows as Pierre. Pierre started to lift weights with Roscoe weeks before going to college, believing he could rush the swollen look. It never happened, so Pierre ended up keeping his natural cut which doesn't look bad at all. Pierre had hoped to gain more female fans with a bulkier body when he left for college since his natural appearance was too regular while his personality leans on popular nerd. Thus, he hopes to start back working out harder this summer in the gym.

"What's up, Pierre, man? What's good? You still lifting those weights or what?" he asks, punching him lightly in the chest. "You look a bit weak in there, homey."

"Just push ups and sit ups, Roscoe," he laughs. "This summer though, I'm with you at the bench just to get a head start. Are you still at the college doing physical therapy...or that sports therapy stuff for the athletes?"

"I still assist. I'm holding off on becoming a therapist until I can save more money. Not feeling the loans or losing what I've already acquired trying to pay for school."

Roscoe is what can be called a young man that carves his own destiny without the debt. Most of his family worked hard to pay for everything they own in cash, and he knows no other way. He refuses to learn another way either. From his car, clothes, food and even his house, although he inherited the money to pay for it from a deceased uncle, was all paid in cash. Roscoe is debt-free, educated and highly attractive to the ladies. All these qualities are great, but even before Roscoe had all the money and the brawn, Maria always had a thing for him. It's always been obvious, and Roscoe knows it. Before today, Maria didn't have enough confidence to say anything directly to him about it, but today is different. She's celebrating her twentieth birthday, and all age limitations are off the table because the word teen no longer exists in her make.

Instead of speaking to Roscoe immediately, Maria keeps quiet. She's well aware of the fact that Roscoe is broken up with his ex as of four months ago, and she's ready for him to see her in a new, more adult, light. Keeping the beauty and charm about herself, she takes a sip of her soda, and then, when she feels Roscoe's eyes on her, she finally looks up from the side and speaks.

"Hey, Roscoe. How ya' been?" she winks as she gives him an extremely obvious glance over from toe to head.

23

Roscoe notices the way she's eyeballing him, but answers in a less seductive manner than Maria has already given him. "I've been good, Maria. What about you? It's good to see you being that I don't see you around much." Although Roscoe is faking like he doesn't notice, he is well aware of the sensual attitude and posture Maria is bringing to the table. Being no novice to women, Roscoe, while looking directly into her eyes, already goes from cleavage to her smile without one single flinch, and he gives all of what he sees a ten. Still, he doesn't let her know.

"Yeah, I'm working, full-time now, at Glynn's Stays."

"Oh, at the hotel uptown."

"That's the one," she confirms, sitting back in her seat. "I decided to take off two full weeks for this feel good vacation with everyone now that we're all back together again. Where's Janet? Is she not coming?"

Janet is Roscoe's ex, and Maria is simply pulling at strings, trying to figure out if his expression or demeanor changes when she says the ex's name. She knows full well that Janet is nowhere around because she and Roscoe broke up a while back. In her mind, how Roscoe answers the question will reveal whether or not he's still attached to his past and not willing to at least try to move into a better future, mainly with her.

Roscoe doesn't flinch when Maria mentions his ex-girlfriend. In fact, he behaves as if he didn't even hear her ask what he considers a prank question by turning his attention to Séa. "Séa, girl! Gimme some."

She reaches over and slides her hand atop his for more of a light hand shake. "It's great to see you, Roscoe. Are you certain you're not going to change your mind at the last minute about this trip? You know how you are most times," she laughs, "In one minute and then out the next." Her eyes switch from Roscoe onto her boyfriend who just happens to be checking his phone and doesn't catch her glance. By the look on his face, it's his mom who checks on him every two hours which, at times, frustrates him. Séa seems a bit uneasy, but she takes a deep breath and then blows her uneasiness off, hoping for a peaceful trip.

"No," he explains, taking another quick look at Maria, but just as quickly moving his attention back to Séa, "There won't be any back tracking. I'm all in, all in," he continues, feeling Maria's eyes on him. He doesn't play into her, however, no matter how attractive he notices she is today. Instead, he takes a seat in the booth adjacent to Séa and Levi, and tosses a stirring straw into his mouth. A waitress comes his way, but Roscoe holds up his hand to let her know that he won't be getting anything.

"Yo, Roscoe," Levi calls, turning his phone off, "Go ahead and grab some grub." He sits back down. "We're not leaving until about twelve, gotta head out to...oh hell naw!" Levi's slumps down into his seat quickly as he watches a nightmare about to unfold.

"Oh no, Levi, what?" Séa asks, springing her head up from beginning to file down her broken nail. When she looks out of the window, she sees two police cars, then she stares directly into her boyfriend's eyes. "Levi, what did you do?"

"I ain't do shit, Séa. Just took some junk food for the ride, no biggy. I always do that. Pigs must've peeped my ride on camera and still don't realize it's just me. Dang," he complains, shaking his head.

"Levi, they're looking in your car! What the hell did you do that for? We have money!"

"Here...use this to bail me out in case it gets that deep."

"What?" Séa asks stressed out while grabbing the money that Levi is shoving near her pants' pocket.

"You heard me," he whispers, not wanting to alert any passers-by of the stash of cash he just gave to Séa. "I left that shit it the damn car. Vacation starts tomorrow playa's, but if you hurry and get me, we can be on the road by tonight. This is some misdemeanor shit, nothing felonious about this. Watch." Levi gets up after kissing Séa on the cheek, but before he even gets to the door, the cops spot him through the window, meeting him before he sets foot on the concrete. The cops aren't even surprised. They are well aware of who he is, and Levi starts in as Séa sits embarrassed.

"I'm gonna tell you, officer. My bad, I forgot!"

"Come on, Levi," the officer, "You didn't forget. You do this all the time. Pay when you pick up. Those are the rules of society."

"Are you really gonna handcuff me? Come on, now," Levi complains as his voice grows distant after the door closes behind him. Séa begins to anger while Roscoe places his hand on her shoulder for comfort. Pierre simply stares out of the window in disgust because he already knows that Levi thought he was being funny when he took the snacks. He does it all the time to Mrs. Woodshell, the owner of the store who has known them since they were much younger, but this time, she's had enough and called the law it seems.

"He's always playing!" Pierre shouts, pissed by the whole situation. He has had to tolerate Levi's antics longer than anyone, and he is ready to throw in the towel and rags. "Now we have to go bail him out...oh and look, there we go! More drama!" He slams himself down into the seat next to Maria again, and they all watch as Mrs. Woodshell drives up in her Lincoln and climb out of the car just so that she can scold Levi.

"That's a wrap," Roscoe concurs, staring out of the window as well, along with the few customers in the restaurant.

"It never fails, Roscoe, man. We need to set off before dark, and now we have to go get him out of jail over probably some chips and cookies."

"No, there were bagels, two chocolate bars, and a water. If I would've known he stole them, I would've made him drive all the way back to give her the money because we don't have time for this," Séa suggests, but no one believes her story about not knowing Levi took the items. She's always taking up for Levi when she shouldn't and slamming him when it really doesn't matter.

27

This is one of those times it mattered, and she's pretending that she has no idea he stole something small from the store. "He passed me some money. I'll get him out if I have to do so. You guys know his uncle isn't going to let him stay in there, and Mrs. Woodshell just wants to teach him a lesson. He'll be out, and we'll be on the way tonight in the car we rented."

"A car? You must mean more than a car, Séa, because it's a huge SUV." Pierre clarifies, already excited to get away in what he considers the best SUV out.

"You mean that Expedition I drove by in his yard?" Roscoe asks.

"You saw it? Huge! We can really relax on the road in that caveman's ride," Pierre responds while envisioning future moments on the road. "For a minute, I thought we would have to drive two cars, but now this will really be a trip to remember."

"Well, come on guys. Let me go ahead and go to the station. I'm gonna call his uncle so we can make this fast," Séa states, rising up from the booth seat. "Everyone can park their cars at my house. My folks will be home. They never go anywhere. That way, we can all leave in one shot after I get back. I'll call my folks to make room in the backyard, so go home and grab your stuff if you don't already have it. I'll meet you all there later." Séa's parents are well off, and each one of their cars can fit in the backyard easily with room to spare. Séa's mom is a full-time teacher and her dad founded and runs a major art gallery downtown. Although they have much, they never raised Séa to feel she's better than anyone else due to money or material things.

Maria stands up, pulling her arms behind her back in a shoulder blade stretch. "Let's get this show on the road." She follows Séa out the door, purposely grazing Roscoe's table with the side of her thigh. He notices and smiles from the corner of his mouth. "Happy birthday, Maria."

"Thanks," she smiles with a wink.

Pierre doesn't say a word, choosing to ignore what he considers to be dumb, open ended conversation for more than one reason.

Chapter Two

"I told ya'll there was nothing to worry about. My girl Séa knows how to pull through for me. Nothing to it," Levi brags after being let out of the cell after being taught a lesson. No charges were filed against him, but he had to sit there for hours for trying to be a petty thief and a jokester at the same time.

"I swear he's got to be an informant with the way he's always in jail but never gets time."

"Informing who about what?" Levi asks, shutting the door behind him as he steps into the SUV that's about to take them deep into the campgrounds on the other side of the state. When the door shuts, he continues to wait on Pierre to answer his question, but since Pierre keeps his mouth closed, Levi continues, "That's what I thought. Ain't none of ya'll committing any acts of treason anytime soon, are you? If so, let me know so I can go pick up that money from the government since I'm such a snitch. If I'm gonna rat something, trust that there's a whole lot of cash behind it. Yeah, I will definitely play snitch for cash. Believe that."

"Let's just go, already! I'm excited! It's already six thirty in the evening, and we can be halfway there as the dusk is settling in if we drive fast enough. It looks like it's about to rain, so let's get a move on. Maria, you got all your stuff, girl?" Séa squeals from the passenger's seat, bouncing up and down on the leather.

Maria, who sits right behind her with Roscoe on the other end, answers, "I have everything I need, chica." She leans forward and whispers into Séa's ear, "And then some," she says referring to Roscoe who already has his eyes shut and ready for this journey. Séa simply shakes her head.

"Everybody should have between five to seven hundred dollars per person. That would give us at the least twenty five hundred dollars for the two weeks. Since we should have all our clothes and two coolers full of meat, we're all set, right, Roscoe, man?" Levi stares through the rear view mirror at him as he sits with his eyes closed, and then cuts his eyes back to the road ahead a little annoyed at the sight of Roscoe catching naps a the start of the trip. "Ain't no sleeping on this trip." He then puts the gear in drive.

Roscoe answers with a thumbs up, keeping his eyes shut, not ready to give Levi the satisfaction of opening his eyelids.

"Then let's ride." Levi pulls off from his house, the last place they had to stop so he could collect his items for the road after getting released from jail. As his mom looks on from the window waving, he shouts across Séa through the passenger's side window, "Love you, mom! I'll bring you something back!"

"Oh gosh!" Séa exclaims, rolling up the window. "Just go. Your mom is probably happy you're leaving so she can get some time away from you after this last stunt.

You keep pushing your luck, and it's gonna run out, babe. Just because you have family in law enforcement doesn't mean that one day you won't have to serve real time."

"Shoot, girl. My ma loves me more than you do, and look at you." He slants his eyes over at her. "Even you hate to be away from me, and that's why you're sitting right here with me, spending this quality time," he grins the sexy way he always does when he kids with her. Séa pretends that she doesn't like it, but she blushes each time. "My mom loves herself some me. I'm her only son." He grabs the rear view mirror, turning it so that he can yell at the others in the back. "The rest of ya'll clowns just mad you had to share that lovin' from your parents with other siblings. Nothing wrong with being rotten like me, hell. I love my moms and my law enforcing family," he smiles.

Maria thumps a piece of hard candy into the back of his head.

"Hey! This ride ain't mine. That'll be five dollars if it stains the seat," Levi complains, rubbing the back of his head while Séa laughs. Then, they hit the road.

Before leaving the city, they all agree to turn off the destination road for a quick stop at the cemetery. It was just last year they lost a member of their crew. Her name was Justynn, and she was only twenty years old when her body was found underneath a car wreck created by a drunk driver. She was riding her bike, as usual, on the way to her job when out of nowhere, instead of yielding to her right of way at the crossing, the car barreled ahead, ramming into her and a tree. Justynn ended up caught underneath the car. She died on the scene.

Justynn used to have a motto about living your life, allowing nothing to get in the way of any good dreams. She was always one to remind everyone of the good in life and to toss the evil because life is far too short and beautiful to waste on nonsense. Justynn wasn't born with everything and every situation in the right place, but her mom told her that she should still move forward, against all odds to create her own odds. This was what Justynn did which is why she rode a bike, got dressed, washed and all with one arm including worked harder than anyone else as a waitress. After her death, her mom carved the words *keep going against all odds* into her tombstone, and this has been everyone's reminder ever since.

Justynn's tombstone is located close to the cars' pathway when driving through the cemetery, so it's easy to spot. There are fresh flowers in a vase that sits there stationary in the cement while Justynn lies beneath the feet of her friends, covered in dirt.

"It's always eerie coming out here," Pierre states as he looks around. The clouds have already started darkening along with the sky.

Levi tosses him a glance as he picks a weed from the ground, placing it in his mouth. "What's so eerie about it? Look around. This is us, man. May as well get used to it while we live, ya' know." He shrugs and smiles off the idea of the cemetery being eerie which is normal for him. It's his own unique way of dismissing his true feelings.

"That's not funny," Séa complains while nudging him. She's not ever settled when at a cemetery, no matter if she's standing underneath her tall, fearless boyfriend, so she prefers to not hear the death jokes, smart remarks or prophecies into an inevitable future of resting in peace. "All I want to do is pay my respects to Justynn and leave. After all, we are going on this vacation partially for her and what she stood for."

Maria kneels down next to the tombstone and rubs the ground with her fingers, the dust rising up over her manicured fingernails. When the tears begin to fall from her eyes, she silently stands back up to walk to the SUV where Roscoe is still standing, having not followed them to the grave. Instead, he chooses to keep his distance until he sees them follow suit behind Maria and walk his way. This is when Roscoe makes his way to the grave, passing everyone else on the way there.

As they pass, Maria catches Séa staring at Roscoe in what she considers a strange way, but before more seconds go by, Séa catches herself and changes the course of her attention. When she notices that Maria is staring back at her wondering what's up, Séa makes up something rather quickly to throw her off of what may really be on her mind. "Why does he do that?" Séa asks.

"Do what?" Maria asks.

"Choose to go there alone so much. I mean, even with us, he's not comfortable."

Maria interjects while wiping her eyes and holding herself in an embrace while scrutinizing Séa over the question, "It's hard for him to show his emotion, especially in front of others." Then, she looks back at Roscoe who stands directly on top of Justynn's grave. "There's nothing wrong with that. He's just like that, Séa. No big deal. What kind of dumb question was that?"

Roscoe hears them chattering about him which causes him to glance up only to spot Maria again, staring him in the face. Instead of continuing to discuss Roscoe with Maria who is under his spell, Séa gladly drops the subject and hops into the SUV to ignore Maria's whole defend Roscoe bit. About three seconds afterward, Maria jumps in as well.

"I miss that girl. We have to do this vacation up for her because she doesn't have the chance to go with us. She would have enjoyed this," Maria continues in remembrance of Justynn.

"It's what she always wanted, for us to all hang out, stop all the bickering. She reminded me of one of those peace for all people, ya know," Séa chimes in.

"Yeah, like a we are the worlder. She was amazing, and no matter what, we could all call on her," Levi says, delivering his perspective on the deceased as he starts up the SUV.

"But let's stop talking about it. If we are going to have a good vacation, let's do it. The one thing Justynn wouldn't want us talking about is her death," Maria says as she examines Roscoe while he walks back to the car. Before he is able to touch the handle of the door, however, he retreats, and Maria grabs the window. "Roscoe!"

"Oh shit!" Pierre shouts. He plasters his face against the back window, watching Roscoe as he draws his jagged-edged blade. From the driver's seat, all Levi can see is Roscoe go into defense mode by pulling out his knife, so he immediately leaps from behind the wheel, ripping his pistol from underneath the seat.

Slithering from underneath the SUV, a huge snake, a Water Moccasin, comes after Roscoe on a mission to harm. The snake is barely visible due to the uncut grass, and it's dark enough on the ground so that no shadows can be seen. Roscoe keeps a keen eye on the reptile despite the darkness, placing several feet in between him and snake, remaining cool as usual. As soon as Levi turns the corner, all the coolness disappears as the pistol goes off three times. Roscoe ducks back as the snake dies in front of SUV after being hit by bullets.

"Anybody want a belt?" Levi looks back into the Expedition as Maria, Pierre and Séa all gawk back at the scene. Roscoe puts his knife back into his pocket, and he and Levi walk back to the ride.

"Thanks, man. It came out of nowhere from underneath the car." Roscoe explains, hopping into the SUV while Levi does the same.

"Ashes to ashes then, right?" Levi states under his breath.

"Yeah, ashes to ashes." Roscoe responds, staring back at Levi harshly but without anyone taking notice, including Levi. He then gets into the seat, buckles up, and they leave the cemetery as it starts to rain.

Chapter Three

As Levi drives down the road, the music plays on low as Séa paints her toe nails, Maria slips in and out of her nap, and Pierre plays cards with Roscoe. Although everything is at peace inside the Expedtion, the tumultuous rain pours down relentlessly on the vehicle. It pours so hard that it weakens Levi's ability to see the road directly in front of him. The wind starts to blow the Expedition sporadically side to side on the back road, so much so that Séa's fingernail polish dumps over onto the floor board.

"Damn. Sorry, Levi," she sighs, lifting it up quickly. "My nail polish remover is in the bag."

"Forget that nail polish. I can't see anything in front of me. Do you see how slow I'm driving, and the force of this wind won't give me a break? Think there's a tornado or something in the area?"

"No, but then again, I wouldn't know for sure. Who knows what could be going on? I'll try to find out what it is on another station." She leans forward to search for the weather, but as she does, she knocks her head into the dashboard after the Expedition lets out a loud noise and the steering wheel jerks, causing Levi to slam on the brakes, sending the deck of cards in between Roscoe and Pierre flying to the front.

"Ay mi Dios! What was that?!" Maria awakens in a shock, holding on to the seat tightly even though her seatbelt is on. When no one answers, she nervously shouts, "Levi!"

"I think we caught a flat, people. Hold tight."

"How the hell can we have caught a flat tire in an Expedition? Aren't they the thickest tires in the world?" Maria screams.

Pierre leans forward and taps Maria on the shoulder in an attempt to make her feel better. "Try to stay calm, Maria. It's cool. Just a flat tire is all."

Instead of paying Pierre any attention, though, Maria peeps over at Roscoe who has already taken off his seatbelt, ready to grab the wheel if need be, but Levi has already moved the car over to what he thinks is the side of the road based off of the change of gravel he feels under the truck. Suddenly, a violent wind blows against the truck causing it to shake as Levi puts on the brake and the emergency lights.

Roscoe chimes in as he tightens his grip on the front seats to stabilize himself. "It's not gonna be safe right here, man, on the side of the road like this in the dark and rain. If we can't see, no one can see. Let me jump out and case the road just to see how far over we are and if there's a place we can ride to in the meantime on this bad wheel. We can't change this tire with the weather like this anyway."

"You're right, man. Damn eighteen wheeler might come and knock the hell out of us on this barren road. Door's unlocked. I'll get out with you. Excuse us, ladies," he says as both he and Roscoe climb over Séa and Maria to get out on the safest side.

"You two are gonna get soaked and sick," warns Séa as she pushes her door open to let Levi out.

"Taking it for the team, baby." Levi kisses her cheek before he hops out.

Roscoe jumps from his back door before Levi, and when they both hit the ground, it isn't three seconds before they disappear behind the blanket of rain. Pierre checks both windows but sees absolutely nothing due to the pounding downpour and the pitch blackness of the night. He then takes the initiative to roll down his window to see if he can hear anything, but nothing, resulting in him rolling the window back up before flooding the whole side of his seat.

"If they aren't back in five minutes, I'm gonna have to go out," he explains.

"You, too? And what if they get back before you do? Do you even know where we are? The navigation system is good and all, but it surely can't change a flat or drive in the dark," Maria states. "You could get turned around out there, and the last thing we need is you to get lost in the middle of this nowhere."

"Yeah, Pierre. Sit tight. They'll be back. We need you right here because if something does happen like they get lost or hurt out there, you're the only one we know with a strong arm for a tire change," Séa explains. "I would call his phone, but there's no signal out here in this middle of nowhere. Besides that, if he answered, his phone would get soaked in this monsoon."

While Séa is talking, Maria's arm slams against the truck as it starts to shake violently. Pierre catches himself on the window while Séa holds on to her seatbelt and pushes the automatic locks on all the doors.

"What the hell is that? Could somebody please tell me what the fuck is shaking this damn truck because it can't be wind that's for damn sure?" Pierre yells, but the girls are screaming non-stop because the truck won't stop shaking. "Hey! Hey! Stop shaking the damn truck!" Pierre rams his foot into the side of the door and the movement stops, leaving just the sound of the wind, rain and a huge gash in the side of the door panel. The girls cling to the middle portion of the SUV, afraid of what could be on either side of them while Pierre sits on guard and ready for retaliation against his use of foot force. Only minutes later, Roscoe and Levi yell for Séa to open the doors.

"Crap!" Séa screams, caught off guard by Levi's yelling at her through the door that she jumps to the driver's seat like an experienced stunt girl.

"Open the door! Open it! It's Roscoe and Levi, Séa. Hurry up!" Maria shouts as she manually opens her door to let Roscoe inside. As soon as he climbs in, water dumps all over Maria's shirt and shorts, and she simply freezes in shock. Roscoe, on the other hand, isn't phased by the mess he's made on her because to him, it's just water. Therefore, he continues to move over to his seat, removing his shirt in the process, which calms Maria, causing her to do the same thing with her own shirt. When Roscoe looks back up, he simply smiles at Maria who is now only wearing a cut off tank top that's barely wet, saved from being drenched like the other shirt she just removed. During their stripper moments, Pierre stares ahead at them, quite disgusted with the whole flirtation in the middle of a crisis.

"Well, what did you guys see?" he asks as Levi finally takes his seat, wetting the entire front end, including Séa's hair because he leaned over her entire body when he climbed inside, nearly tripping, making her furious.

"Man, we're still halfway in the road, but there's a pathway to the right of us that doesn't even show up on the navigation system. We can ride inside on the busted wheel because it's literally right there." He points. "There's a blanket of trees that blocked some of the rain so we could see a bit better. We can get in there and chill until this lets up, maybe even change the tire," Roscoe explains.

"Was that you and Levi shaking the truck? If so, warn a brother first because that was some scary shit."

Levi turns around. "Shaking the truck? Man, do you really think that me and Roscoe, in all this weather, would be outside shaking this big ass SUV for fun? Roscoe already said what we were doing and what we found, now sit tight. Shaking some damn truck..." he mumbles under his breath, already pissed off that he's soaked from head to toe.

"No seriously, Levi, the truck was shaking," Séa seethes, "And it wasn't the wind. It was like someone or something was trying to tip it completely over, and it just happened to stop right before you and Roscoe got back to the door," she complains with her fingers in the quote end quote symbols.

Levi starts up the vehicle, visibly about to burst into an all outrage. He gives her the side eye, trying his absolute best not to blow a fuse, but it comes out anyway. "I just went outside in the pouring rain to come back in and hear this - about some damn rocking rental? I'm gonna tell you this once and for all, Séa. I didn't shake this Expedition and neither did Roscoe. Don't you know the wind is blowing? Hell, I have to pay for damage to this big ass load…and you do, too," he points to everyone behind him. "One hundred dollars each for every piece of this truck harmed. I'm glad it's leather in this beast. Now let's ride under these trees until this blows over, and chill with these assi-damn-nine accusations."

"Some start to the vacation," complains Pierre quietly to himself as he lies back onto the seat, watching Levi pull slowly into what feels like a dip leading to whatever side road they were talking about.

The further the group moves onto the side road, the more visible the scenery becomes due to the huge trees that are diverting the heavily falling rain. From behind, Pierre watches rain drench the back windshield until the SUV rolls underneath the umbrella of trees, allowing him to make out a gated entrance. He also notices a portion of a sign that's tilted off on the edge of the gate, but can't see the entire sign.

"Where are we?" Pierre asks. "What is this place?"

"We just need to pull in here because we don't know what's out there on the road. After the rain stops, we'll change the tire and head out. No big thing, man. Chill." Roscoe is obviously getting irritated with Pierre's whining and everyone else appears to be a bit ticked as well. Pierre has always been very particular, and when he's under stress, he likes to have every T crossed. This is one of those moments.

"Is it someone's residence? We can't just pull up into someone's home, change a tire on their property like it's all good."

Levi looks back through the rear view mirror at Pierre who is still anxiously awaiting an answer to what he feels is a very valid question. "Peanuts," he pauses, "when we pull up to the house or community back here, then we will figure all that out. Bottom line is that we can't go far with this wheel, and unless you want to walk back home in the rain, shut the hell up and grow some balls, man."

"Alright," Pierre nods his head but in a great deal of disgust, ready to confront Levi for continuing to bully him. "Alright, keep it up. I'm tired of your crap, Levi, so keep it up."

Roscoe puts his hand up slightly as to calm Pierre down while he checks out the landscape around them. So far, there's nothing to be seen but trees, trees and more trees as the lights from the Expedition are on high beam. There are gaps in between the leaning trees of about six feet, but besides the road that they are driving down, there are no signs that any residence even exists until Roscoe finally spots it as Levi turns carefully with the curve, beyond a mountain of unkept bushes and vines.

Levi drives slowly around a downed tree that lays near the center of the dirt road, and once he clears it, there are three homes, two story homes that sit side by side cul-de-sac style, but each one of them appear abandoned. As everyone strains to look around in the dismal weather, Levi cautiously pulls to a stop dead center all three of the run down looking homes.

"It doesn't look like anyone lives here, people," Levi sighs. "What do you think? I don't see any cars or signs of people who really care about their lives over here," he asks, glancing over at Séa who is busy debating about what she sees through the rain.

"It looks old and nearly rotted out. No one can possibly live here on a continual basis. There's absolutely no way. You think we should go knock just in case?" She stares backwards at the others who are obviously wondering what to do next. "Well? What do you guys think? Should we go ring a bell or something because I can't get any signal on my phone, and the only form of communication we have right now with this blown tire is to physically walk and talk. I don't want us to get attacked for trespassing or anything."

"It looks like we got no choice, Séa," Maria replies, with an uneasy appearance to her face. "There's something weird about this place though…like I know it from somewhere."

"It's called déjà vous. Every human being alive has it at one point or another, so don't get your

46

suspicious ass all up in arms about nothing. Roscoe, you coming, man? Pierre, hit up the house on the end."

"You don't wanna wait until this rain stops?" Pierre asks. Then, everyone glances at him with a blank stare. "What?" he asks defensively as Maria grabs his hand to emphasize that now isn't the time for his dramatics, but he continues to talk. "If you ask me, I would've taken my chances on the side of the road."

"Pierre, just go. We just need to be sure we aren't on private property just like you said, remember? Would you like people to pull up in your yard and change a tire?" Pierre doesn't respond, so Maria continues. "Just go already, geesh."

"Don't say shit, Levi. I was just saying. The rain may stop soon is all, but I got you. My bad," he complains apologetically for acting like a wimp as he opens the door and steps out of the vehicle with a shirtless Roscoe to follow. Levi then hops out of the driver's seat, leaving Maria and Séa inside. Maria continues to kiss the locket hanging from her necklace, apprehensive about the whole journey thus far.

"Why are you so scared acting, Maria? Things are fine. Levi is right. You're just too superstitious, girl!" she explains, tossing a pack of ketchup directly at her. "Look at the way those houses look in the dark. Imagine what they look like in the day. Trust...no one lives here. This place has to be abandoned."

"No one's scared, Séa. I just don't like to feel familiar with a place when I don't know why I feel familiar with it is all. That spooks me out, but it doesn't scare me.

There's a difference." She answers, continuing to peer out through the rain that is still coming down heavily while the debris flies by in the distance. "Is there a tornado or something coming out here? This wind is no joke." Then she squints to get some sign from the sky but sees nothing. "I'm not trying to be sucked up in a damn cloud."

Séa turns to watch the guys outside as they wait on a response, each one at a different front door. When she turns back to Levi, she notices that he's no longer standing outside on the porch.

"Crap, Maria," she says, leaning over closer to the windshield and speeding up the windshield wipers. "Stupid! Stupid! Stupid!"

"What?" Maria jumps to the front seat quickly, landing on the driver's side.

"It's damn Levi. He's not on the porch," she responds, lifting her shirt over her hair, preparing to make a run for it outside. "I think his dumb ass went in. That's all we need right now is him getting a charge for doing something that appears like a home invasion when in reality, it's his dumb butt being silly again."

"He took his gun?"

Séa rolls her eyes in disbelief that Maria doesn't know Levi a bit better than to not tote his firearm, especially in the middle of only God knows where. "He never leaves home without it, and we are far away from his house right now. Check beneath the seat."

48

Maria rubs her hand underneath the bottom of the driver's seat, and she feels no gun. "Oh no, Séa."

"Oh yeah. Let's hope I'm right about this place being abandoned. Just because it *looks* empty doesn't mean it is empty because if it's not, we're all about to spend time in prison for absolutely nothing." Séa jumps from the SUV, and a hesitant Maria follows behind after removing the keys from the ignition. The rain beats atop their heads as they fail to dodge the downpour no matter how fast they run, and as soon as they reach the porch's covering, they let out a sigh of relief.

"Levi!" Séa calls as she now notices that the house is completely empty besides some old unused furniture, but her boyfriend is nowhere to be seen from where she's standing. Maria reaches out to grab Séa's arm when she notices that Séa is about to cross the threshold.

"No, stupid! Don't just follow Levi blindly! What's wrong with you?"

"Girl, he has to come up out of there. He's probably getting into something else that will potentially ruin our vacation, Maria." She removes her arm from Maria's grasp and continues, "Think about it? When hasn't Levi been the one to ruin a party?"

"Now that you say that…" she states, tossing her long, wet hair to the side to ring it out.

Roscoe runs up underneath the porch with Séa and Maria while Pierre ends up in a frustrated stroll back to the SUV, not trying to fight the rain at all. Roscoe calls out, "Hey, Pierre, over here, man. Let's go up in here until this storm is over."

"So all the houses are empty, huh?" Maria asks.

"Yeah, baby," he answers, making Maria melt inside, although he didn't mean anything by it. He calls all the females he's familiar with baby, but Maria takes it as an exclusive flirt. "What are we standing out here for?"

"Maria wouldn't let me go in after Levi. She's scared."

"Let's go," Roscoe commands, leading the way as his footsteps create more wet prints over the ones left by Levi. Pierre hops onto the porch, the last one in the house, shutting the heavy, wooden door behind him as Maria and Séa ease slowly inside.

Upon entry, a loud crackle of thunder sounds off from the sky. The floors shake with each step as the hardwoods beneath their feet are rotted out so badly that there's a definite possibility that they may cave in. There's no polish anywhere on the old, grimy furniture. Every part of the house appears to have been overcome by buckets of dust and walls of webs atop the fact that there are no reflections in the mirrors.

"Look at this filth," Séa whispers to herself as she becomes disgusted by the heavy, slimy film that covers the mirror like a blanket. Maria notices what she is describing, picks up a stick, and then scrapes it across the mirror's glass only to remove a portion of the dirt and grime that covers it. Then, she begins to scrape the mirror vigorously until she is able to see strips of her reflection.

"This place is nothing short of a germ dwelling." Then, she drops the stick to bring on the urgency of Levi's return to the front of the house. "Levi, come on!" she yells as she looks back a Pierre who she can tell is just as uncomfortable as she is. "This place is spooking me out." Maria continues to move toward the middle of the floor, searching for the root of her anxiety but falls short as she takes in all the dust resulting in a fit of coughing.

Pierre, growing the courage Levi continues to tell him he needs, decides to be a comfort instead of a cop out, therefore, instead of agreeing with Maria, he tries to calm her. "It's not that bad. At least we can dry off a bit in here, and then, change clothes later because you never know what's out there right now. We're somewhat safer in here..." He spot checks the room visually by moving his glasses further away from his face, causing things to get bigger. "Well, I really don't know how much safer, but it's drier at least."

Roscoe is already on the stairs, heading to the second floor because to the dirty, eroded carpet is where Levi's footprints lead, but when he gets halfway up, Levi leaps out from the doorway entrance that's right beside Séa causing her to fall back against Maria in a horrifying scream.

"Levi!" Séa yells as she reaches up and slugs him in his shoulder, "with your stupid ass!"

"Ouch, baby! That hurt. What'd you do that for?"

In a rage, Séa responds, "We've been calling you since you've been in this old shack, but you never answered and your damn footsteps went to the staircase! Stop trying to scare people, damn, Levi."

"What footsteps? My footsteps?" Levi asks looking to his right only to find Roscoe halfway up the staircase but walking back down.

"Levi, don't act stupid. Yes, your footsteps. We just came in behind you and thought you were upstairs."

Levi looks at the floor and locates the footsteps that Séa is talking about while Roscoe plants his feet back on the weak, wooden bottom floor, shaking his head at Levi but refraining from commenting on what he believes is another one of Levi's jokes gone wrong. Levi catches a glance from Roscoe, senses the negative vibe coming off of him, but chooses to ignore what he understands as a diss. Instead, he addresses his girlfriend Séa.

"I didn't even walk over there, Séa," he says calmly. "When I came in the door, my feet couldn't have had that much water on them anyway because I dried them off on that big ass mat that I kicked by the door when I saw a filthy water bug trying to give me rent money for this dump." Then, he points to the footprints on the floor. "Those are fresh out of the water, just like Roscoe's."

Séa doesn't stick around to argue, but starts to walk back toward the front door. "You're so full of shit."

Levi tosses his arms out to his sides. "Aren't we all? I mean that in the literal way, though, Séa." He pauses to check if everyone else believes his story, but the looks on their faces are identical to Séa's – like they're sick of his bad jokes. "Séa, what are you going back outside for? We can't do anything but sit in the truck. Instead of going back out there and getting drenched, let's check this place out. I found some old Pepsi's back here in the back, you know like in the bottle." He demonstrates the length of them with his hands, but when no one gets excited, he rushes over in front of Séa who stands only three feet from the front door. "We can either go back out here," he offers as he turns the knob slowly. Séa just stands there with her hands folded as Levi eventually swings the front door wide open, only to expose the furious weather outside, worse than when they pulled up only minutes ago. The rain begins to pour inside the old house, and that's when Séa shoves him out of the way and shuts the door herself, turning her back to the outside scene.

"Okay, Levi. You win." She looks around at Maria who is overtly upset at position everyone is in. "What do you say, Maria? We may as well dry off inside here instead of sitting soaked inside the SUV for only the heavens know how long."

Maria isn't convinced, but she agrees anyway. "As long as we all stay together..."

Levi walks over in front of her, cutting her off mid sentence. "Maria."

"What?" she asks, although she already knows that Levi is going to have something to say about her being superstitious.

"Boo!" he taunts, throwing his arms up in the air and arranging his fingers like claws. "Stop being so damn scary." Then, he moves toward the doorway from where he jumped out and frightened Séa. "Ain't crap in here but us, my pistol, and exploration for a minute. Let's do it. Isn't that why we left home together, so that we can explore and live beyond what we normally do. We may as well start the vacation from here."

"Just don't try anymore dumb shit, Levi," Pierre complains.

Levi stares back at the footsteps on the floor that he was accused of making. "I said that I didn't do that shit." Then he turns and points toward the doorway right in front of him which leads to the kitchen. "I went this way, not that way." Then he grins again. "You swear somebody's trying to scare the hell out of you, and that's not even the case. Balls...grow some. I'ma make a man outta you yet, Peanuts."

As they drag themselves through the doorway behind Levi, the size of the kitchen overwhelms them along with the stains and grease they find layered on everything from the counters to the cabinets. Roscoe rubs his thumb over the countertop, uncovering brown and white tiles. Pierre reaches up and peels open a cabinet that reveals canned foods, neatly arranged and in order.

"Wow. Whoever lived here used to be a neat freak. Too bad they left because this place looks like...wait. Check this out, guys." Pierre walks over to a center table that's not center anywhere but more shoved into the corner near a foggy window. "This is a famous spot! The grand opening is framed in this newspaper clipping. We're walking on history."

"Lemme see that," Levi walks over, snatches the frame off the table and blows the settled dust off. He smirks, turns and then speaks, "I'll be damned. This place was really in the paper, opened before we were all born. Looks like we hit the jackpot. Probably some collector's shit in here somewhere along with those Pepsi bottles," he pauses, "Ain't that right, Roscoe?" Levi asks purposely in a lower tone as to worsen the tension that's been on and off between them since they left the restaurant earlier. He sits the framed newspaper photo back on the table and turns to make his way to a staircase that's around the immediate corner.

"Well, what did the article say? What's the name of this place? What is it?" Séa asks, but Levi is already making his way elsewhere. Therefore, Roscoe, who is consistently ignoring Levi's snide remarks toward him, grabs the frame again to get more information from it.

"It says in the caption that it's some old residence for the homeless. I guess it gives them an address to get started, and according to the piece of paper that isn't ripped off, once they work for six months to a year, they leave with enough money to fend for themselves." He put the frame back down and knocks the wall with his knuckles. "Looks like this place all started with an

55

address for a job application to help people get along in the working world."

"That's pretty cool. It's completely shut down now, but what a really good cause. What was the name of it?" Séa asks, feeling a bit more settled with the news that no one currently lives inside.

"It was cut off, but I saw the word *gates*, but that's it."

"That explains the gates," Pierre adds. "There's a sign back there when we came in."

"Yeah?" Roscoe asked.

"Yeah, but I couldn't see it good because of all the rain. I'm just glad to know that we aren't in any way shape or form about to get arrested for stealing shelter here. This place is probably scheduled to be condemned."

"Either that or be renovated," Séa states. "Let's go." She walks around the corner in the direction of Levi, and Pierre follows. Maria hesitates, grabbing Roscoe by the wrist, holding him back from proceeding ahead.

"Roscoe, I don't know about this. I have a bad feeling," she continues, shaking her hands out in front of her body, "like really bad – almost sick." She waits on him to respond, but she senses that he believes she's doing nothing but the usual flirting, trying to play helpless and scared. Even though Roscoe is wearing no shirt and his muscles are protruding so brilliantly that it would make any warm blooded woman blush, she pretends as if she could care less, continuing to appear as serious as she can. "Roscoe, all jokes aside," she says, looking over her shoulder because she can literally feel the presence of someone watching her. "I don't feel good about this. I really don't. Can we just go back to the truck, or just stay here for that matter..."

Roscoe then reaches over, placing his arm around her shoulders, leading her in the direction of the others. "It's good. I gotcha." He finally notices her hands shaking uncontrollably as she yanks down on her tank top. "You're not bullshittin', are you?"

"No, Roscoe!" she punches him in his stomach playfully. Her punch didn't even make a dent in his well defined abs. "Something isn't right. History, homeless people or whatever that newspaper clipping said, I told you that I have a bad feeling, and that's what it is, comprende?"

"Don't go speaking Spanish on me. I know you change up on your language when you get mad. We're good, and I'm not trying to upset you. Put it like this," he halts to make her face him and listen. "I would go back with you, but it's best that we stay in a group if you're feeling like we're on the wrong track." Then, he slides his hand down her waist and turns her back around. Leaning over to her left ear, he states, "Walk in front of me. I got you back here." He peers ahead to watch the other three go out of sight.

She smiles, a bit more at ease, feeling closer and more secure with him being so connected to her emotions. "I bet you do." Maria then turns back around to reconnect with his naked flesh and eyes. He reaches for Maria's hand, and she takes one step forward while he brings his body as close to hers, an action he's never taken before. Maria melts into a dreamland of only herself and Roscoe, ignoring the fact that she's still inside a dusty dilemma of déjà vu that's creeping her out. As he stares into her eyes and other places that are just as exposed, he tells her, "I got you. Nothing's gonna happen to you today, birthday girl." He lifts her hand into the air and spins her back around, noticing the way she moves, and Maria continues to walk ahead happy for his attention. However, despite her flirtation with her crush, she clings to her locket as she moves up a flight of stairs.

When they make it up the staircase, they find the others looking out into the backyard from a covered balcony, so they join them, walking separately.

"What's this, you guys?" Maria asks, approaching as the rain slows down to a steadier, but still very rapid, pace. No one answers her, so she repeats herself, "Hello? Let me see. Scoot over, Pierre. Let me get in by Séa."

Séa turns around and grabs her by the elbow as Roscoe closes in and sees just what everyone else is visualizing.

"Girl, look! Who would imagine something so profound would be tucked back here in all this forest and bushes, especially behind some homes for the homeless. This really must be some old archive-able place that we just happened to run into. It has to be some museum or something? I can only imagine what's inside!" she exclaims, her eyes bulging out of their sockets. "It's bad ass is all I know, and I want some pictures in front of it right now!"

The building Séa glosses over is made of what looks like cement and stone, however, it is strategically placed directly in the center of a tall mob of beautiful trees with a pathway going back to the three homes. Although the pathway appears to be a complete wreck do to it being unkept, with imagination, all of them can see the art and preparation that went into building a place the size of this. The trees seem to be a way to shield onlookers while the beauty of the front of the building, mainly the entrance, displays a fascinating glow that could uplift any person in despair. Even in the dark, the entrance is magnificent.

"Wow, Séa! It looks like something you see on a movie, a flashy ass cathedral or something – at least that's what the front looks like, but I can barely see the rest. The mist is killer. What time is it?" Maria asks, and Pierre quickly provides the answer, jumping on board with what he feels is a great opportunity for some great camera shots.

"It's only about ten o'clock right now. We can go on over there if you want, seeing as my camera is in the SUV, and we can get photos of both of you and Séa here first before we even get to the vacation spot," Pierre offers. Along with practicing his nighttime photography skills, Pierre is also dying to get Maria to see him as more than just a dork friend that she loves so much. Fact is that Pierre has had his heart set on Maria for years now, unable to reach the level that Maria is attracted to – the Roscoe level. Although he still wants to swell up with the muscles, Pierre also wants Maria to see him for more than just Levi's little cousin and her peer. He wants her to see him for the swag that he brings to the table, not in stature all the time, but in the mind and something he's naturally good at – behind the camera – making anyone look better and more desirable in photo.

"Ain't nobody got time for that, Peanuts, man! Pictures in the rain and fog, Peanuts? Come on, now!"

"Shut up, Levi," he retorts, shoving his cousin against the balcony's edge. "I told you about belittling me, didn't I? Didn't I?" Pierre hollers, with an overcoming rage that has positioned him in a confrontational mode with Levi.

"Oh shit!" Levi yells, catching himself on the rail as Séa grabs his other arm to prevent him from falling over the balcony. Levi is in total shock, shooting a blasting stare at his own cousin in disbelief. "Is your ass fuckin' crazy, Peanuts?" When Pierre stalls on a reply, Levi lunges forward to take Pierre down to the floor, and he does just that. Hitting his head on the ground, Pierre swings at Levi, but misses as Levi rears his arm all the way up in punch mode, and swings. Roscoe intervenes, dropping down on his knees to bring Levi's fist to a flying stop in mid air.

"Get the fuck off me, money! This mother fucker almost knocked my black ass off the balcony, man!" He hollers, staring at Roscoe like a mad man, his eyes gone near psycho. "I said let me go!" Levi yanks his arm away from Roscoe, and they both stand up. Levi's anger is now aimed directly at Roscoe, and Roscoe isn't flinching. "This is my family, and this coward down here," he shouts, shoving Pierre's feet from in front of him, "knows better than to put his hands on me." Then, he walks closer to Roscoe, almost chest to chest, breathing like a mad man ready to take aim at his ex-best friend's face. "And you should know better, too, ain't that right?"

Roscoe's face remains perfectly still, and everyone knows what's about to go down. Maria runs to Pierre's side as he gets up off the floor, while Séa positions herself behind Levi in an attempt to snatch his gun if he reaches for it. He's never drawn on anyone ever before, but because of his past with Roscoe, she's feeling like anything could happen. When she steps behind Levi, her eyes move between Roscoe and the pistol. Her heart pounds as she imagines the death that could occur at any moment.

"You heard me, Roscoe, man? You should know about putting your hands on people, right?" He looks back at Séa as she tugs at the back of his shirt. He fails to retreat as he is nose to nose with a Roscoe who's ready to throw blows if he has to do so, evident by the way his chest is tensing up.

"That's old, Levi. Let that go," Roscoe warns.

"Let it go? I bet you think you can try that same shit, so what the hell you mean let it go? Let you do that shit again? Huh? Is that what you mean?"

Roscoe simply tosses his hands up in surrender, staring behind Levi at a worried Séa, and does what he asked Levi to do – let it go. As he walks from the balcony further into the house, Maria follows along with Pierre while Séa stands by her man, not in defense of him, but just to help him cool down.

"What the hell was that?"

"Séa, don't start in on me," Levi warns her as she continues to force herself in his face as he tries to move away from her.

"No, Levi, cut it out. All Roscoe was trying to do was cool things down. I thought you guys got started on the right foot, especially after the snake incident at the cemetery," she stresses.

Levi's hands clasp together at the back of his head as he glares over at the back of Roscoe as he chats with Pierre and Maria. He's fuming as he paces back and forth on the balcony. Séa awaits a better response from her man who is all about setting things off and setting things straight with his fists all on Roscoe's face.

"Things will never be that straight with us, Séa. That man's always flexing his muscle where he doesn't belong. Look at his half naked ass over there all *swoll* up, the only one prancing his ass around with a shirt off!" Levi states, doing a chicken dance on the balcony. "He knows what the hell he did back in the day. I'm not saying that we'll never be cool, but that shit was foul, and he needs to admit the shit."

"Babe, you're with me now!" Séa shouts, tears rushing up into her eyes out of frustration behind the whole situation. "What do you care about that girl for?"

Levi reaches over and places both of his palms on Séa's teary cheeks. "It's not about the girl, Séa! It's the principle of the thing. Do you get that at all? If Maria came and rubbed her hands all over my chest and you walked up on it, that would be fucked up now wouldn't it?"

Séa doesn't answer, but in the back of her mind, she realizes all the truth coming from Levi's mouth.

"Now you tell me, would it be about me later on down the road with you and her, or would that shit be about principle?" He waits on her to answer, but she doesn't. All she does is shut her eyes and place her fingertips on the corners so her eyes won't look a warm mess when she goes back inside. "That's what I thought, Séa." He pulls her in closer to his chest. "It's the principle. I can't trust that dude. Best friends don't do that to each other. That was my boy, babe. We were like blood."

"Just let it go. You can't tell me that y'all don't have love for each other still...no matter what," she says, glancing over at Roscoe.

"I'm not saying that, Séa. Just let this stay between me and him. That man better not put his hands on me again, and he damn sure better not touch you. Peanuts is my blood. If we tussle..." He shrugs his shoulders. "We tussle. No love lost because blood is always thicker than water. Roscoe better not get it twisted."

"Come on, Levi. Go tap and let it be. For me," she pleads.

He looks at Séa and softens with the knowledge that he really wants her to have a good time. Therefore, he shoves all his anger aside for the moment to fix her saddened emotional state by walking her over while he stands before Roscoe.

"Yo, man, we good?" Levi asks, with a half cocked attitude.

"Ain't nothing, man. We'll talk," Roscoe states, throwing his knuckles out for dap. "I was just trying to help, Levi," he sighs, "You know that."

"Yeah," Levi responds, "But we're gonna leave that trying to help shit over there. No beef from here on out though." Levi then flashes that money making smile that all the girls love. It's one of his most attractive qualities, but in this moment, he's using it as a shield, or a form of deceit, to hide how he really feels.

"Pierre, hey look. That wasn't a bad idea. My bad, man. Go get that camera, and maybe we can get some shots of my fly female after all." He looks over at Maria. "And you can get in, too, Maria. Just don't try to shade the light from my baby over here." He leans in and kisses Séa on the forehead, and she leans her head onto his chest. "After this photoshoot, we'll head out."

"What are you trying to say?" Maria asks in reply to his shade Séa's light comment, realizing happily that the tone of the night is coming back to fun and jokes and not fury.

"Sorry about that, Levi." Pierre apologizes to his older cousin for nearly sending him to his potential death on the balcony. "I wasn't thinking when I pushed you over there so close to the rail."

　　　"Ain't nothin'. Let's go. We're blood, man. Blood," he reiterates, shooting a look back at Roscoe that only they understand as meaning the apology only seconds ago is fake. They still have issues to sort out, but at another time.

Chapter Four

The group makes it back down the stairs, but not the same way they came up. The staircase is a continuous one, causing them to exit back at the entrance to the house where they first followed the wet footsteps.

"I've never been in a house that I can go up one way and go down another," Pierre starts. "I guess that shows how much less money I have than the people who owned this property."

"Me either. It's too bad this house is so old. These homeless people were living it up. I would move in if it wasn't so drab," says Séa. "It's a great steal if it gets cleaned up."

"Yeah. The idea was good for the homeless, but this place probably shut down because of the upkeep, taxes and everything else," chimes in Roscoe who is busy shaking the loose wooden rail. "Plus termite control."

"Tell me about it," says Maria who bounces off of every word he says which gets underneath Levi's skin, but he keeps quiet just to keep Séa happy. "Are you sure your camera equipment won't get wet on our way over there?"

"No, it's good. The rain is down to about a good sprinkle now. Besides that, the place is a hop, skip and a jump. With my equipment being in leather bags, everything will be good. You can change in here, and then we can roll out through the back door, take that pathway, and then we're there. I've been waiting on testing my nighttime shots with the new lens I have, so I'm game," Pierre responds, all geared up and ready, having already pushed the fight between he and Levi out of his mind. This is all he needs to get to spend more time with Maria who has yet to see herself captured by his camera. Séa already knows his work, but this will be Maria's first time. Pierre is betting on her liking the photos so much that she ends up wanting more time with the lens, thus, more time with him. He still hasn't enough courage to dive straight in and ask her for a date due to his own insecurities.

"We need more light for photos and changing, don't we, Pierre? We could barely see at the back of the house, and now that the lights are out in the Expedition, we can't even see in the front."

"Maria, we have flashlights on our cell phones for the small stuff. Plus I have a huge light for the photos. You and Séa can use that. That's a nice spot to take some shots, though," Pierre says looking around having already placed on his fake professional photographer's hat. "It's deserted, but it can make for some great photos, ones that are out of the norm."

"I agree! Let's do it. You know I'm still on my wanna be fashion model kick," Séa exclaims. "Real models have to work in all sorts of weather so bring it.

Shine your light in the house, Pierre, and me and Maria will deck out! Gel and a little Shea Butter will fix my hair, and it's a go!"

There the Expedition is, sitting in the same spot they left it with one extremely flat front tire. As the girls pull out what they consider as their fashionable outfits and Pierre easily grabs his camera bag with tripod and light, Roscoe pulls Levi aside, after grabbing a clean, dry shirt. He takes Levi far enough away from the others so that they can discuss an issue that they haven't spoken about yet without a quarrel.

"Levi, man. I have never tried to lighten this issue for you because it's real as hell. Even though it was a while ago, I can understand why you and me aren't down like that anymore. That girl didn't mean to me what she meant to you, and that was my bad. I messed up, but word on my life, I didn't lay her down man. She laid herself down there, and I played my part in letting her do it. I didn't stop her, and my mind wasn't even on anything like betraying you. I touched her, but that was it. I wasn't about to lay down there with her. I promise you. It's hard to believe, I know, because you walked in before I walked out, but that's law, bro. That's law."

Levi doesn't speak. Instead, he walks slowly around Roscoe who is now taking deep breaths wondering why he even tried to talk one last time to the man who knows all his secrets and vice versa. Roscoe, after standing completely still and allowing Levi to circle him like a bulldog, ends up regretting the whole apology thing.

"Look dude, I'm not about all this walking around me like you're about something, so if you're gonna jump, then jump. We can brawl right now since you've been holding it in for so long. All I'm saying is that I was younger then, and I shouldn't have even looked her way but I did. I'm a man...but I didn't touch her. No matter what she told you, I didn't ... I mean I touched her," he corrects himself, "but that was it. That's as far as it went."

Levi finally makes it back around to Roscoe's face, and looks him square in the eyes. "You fucked up."

"Yeah, I did. What now? From right here, I see you have the woman of your dreams in Séa, right? I learned my lesson, Levi. You may be a lot of things, man, but you're good on your word. I'm just sorry I messed mine up. For real. Now back the hell up off me because you know I don't do that beg a man shit. We can either throw blows, or we let it go. Now is a better time than any." Roscoe spreads his arms out as an invitation to wrestle, but Levi stands down.

"I don't wanna beat your ass out here in front of Maria, so I'll let it go." They slap paws, but Levi adds, "This doesn't mean that I don't have my eyes on you, but, man, look, there wouldn't be nothing like having my road dawg back, you feel me? So are we bros?"

"Yeah, man. That was my bad. I didn't intend on that to happen." He peeps over at Séa and then back at the ground.

"No more, man. Don't do that shit..."

70

"It's done." Roscoe cuts him off. "I've heard that you and Séa are about to tie the knot though," Roscoe assumes over rumors that he's heard through the grapevine.

Levi already knows where the leak came from. "Peanuts and his big mouth, huh?"

"You know it. I talked to him earlier in the year, and he said you mentioned Séa being the one. You think?"

"Man, I'm sure. The only thing I need to be sure of is that I won't mess that shit up. She's way more mature than my ass. I can't marry her and then do the stupid shit I like to do. I still like to do dumb, fun stuff, and she's just so serious most times. I know she loves me though. Who else would tolerate me, man? I know I put her through just about everything, but she knows I'll try to give her the world."

"I feel you. If that's your woman, then it's your woman."

"What about you and Maria, the chica," Levi sings as they walk slowly back toward the SUV, watching the girls take their clothes inside the house as Pierre follows them with the light, case and camera. Levi adjusts his gun on his side just in case as Roscoe scans the woods.

"She's yeah...," he pauses, "She's alright. You know I don't like pushy females. She gotta control that shit before I take her seriously, plus she just turned twenty today. That's officially my age, man."

"Not a teen anymore."

"Full grown. She looks much better, but like I said, she let's me read her like a book."

"You still need that mystery, dude?"

"Ain't shit to chase if it's always in your face. Too clingy."

"True that. True that."

"She'll run my ass away." He wipes his go-tee. "She's on fire though," he says, looking her way as she grins while entering the house. "Yeah, she's on fire, but I just might have to put that fire out. Pierre is..."

"Too slow," Levi interjects. "Like I've been telling him. He needs to man up and ask the girl out. I know he's on her like a rabid dog, but she doesn't know that. The boy couldn't drop a hint if it fell on him!"

They both laugh and make their way to the porch.

"That's good, Pierre, and no peeking!" Maria giggles as she quickly slides on her clothes, pulls her hair up in a tight, high ponytail and proceeds to look in the newly cleaned mirror to put on make-up. She then looks over at Séa who is nearly ready to pose because she decided to keep on her wet shirt but changed into some tight jeans. She also has some super high red heels and black boots to slide on her feet as soon as she gets to the amateur set. "So what do you think? You think he really likes me?" Maria asks, referring to Roscoe.

"Girl, shh!" she responds, slamming her hand over Maria's mouth. "You know Pierre has a super duper crush on you. Don't be so insensitive," she grins, removing her hand. "He's being nice and all, taking pics of us out here in the rain with this dope backdrop, so let up off of Roscoe for a minute. Pierre really digs you." She combs through her short do and layers it in place so that the curls do as ordered. Then, she cuts her eyes over at Maria. "You know he wouldn't have volunteered to do this if you weren't here. He's showing out. When you see him at work with his little photography pastime, you might end up interested in him. Never know. He has that camera swag action going on!"

"Stop lying, Séa. You're starting to get just like your man...always got jokes that aren't funny. Pierre can't be as into me as you say he is. He's been around me forever and never said a word," she stresses, "so that whole crush thing is nothing short of a big lie. He's had plenty time to ask me out, and never, not once, has he done it."

"No, for real. He digs you. Without his jacked up wardrobe, he is kinda cute. Just look at him for a change. For real, just look at him. He's really not that bad minus his corny ways at times."

Maria peeps around the corner at Pierre as he leans on the wall waiting for them as they prepare for the start of their first ever portfolio together. She scans his body, imagining what he may look like underneath all the scruffy clothes and dingy shoes. Then, finally she picks his face apart. After about thirty seconds, she ends her scan of Pierre, only to grab Sea's attention with a final conclusion. "If he straightens himself out a little bit, get a haircut, and change those glasses, he would probably be cute. I just never looked at him that way."

"Well, maybe you should. Levi's family has good genes, you know," she laughs. "Sometimes those genes hide out in the craziest places. He may be a little weird, but if you can't get with Roscoe in the next couple weeks, then give Pierre a shot. He's a little slow on the flirtation end, but you never know. As far as Roscoe, you already know that you're gonna have to put in work with him, so go for the man who already sees the special in you."

"Don't make me vomit," Maria laughs. "Come on. I'm not talking about dating someone I see as my brother. Let's go. We have to get the pics so we can get back on the road before sun up or it starts pouring down heavily again."

Séa looks back at her and smiles. "You're right about getting back on the road. Check this out though, if I wasn't an all natural girl, my hair would be so lame right now, but I know how to rock the wet and curly look like a pro, boo. Check it!" She spins around and lowers her head closer to the light. "She worked that out, didn't she?"

"Yes, she did!"

They slap pinkies and leave the house, the guys following behind as they make their way to the beautiful backdrop of a mysterious building behind the run down shacks, shining their cell phone flashlights the whole way down while it sprinkles.

Chapter Five

"Well, now that we're actually up close and personal to this place, it looks like the only thing beautiful about the building is the front entrance," Maria complains about how the building is so exotic from the front but just plain cement all around which was hard for them to tell in the darkness from the house behind them.

"Yeah," Pierre agrees, placing his bag of camera equipment down next to words that are engraved on the building. He glances over them, but pays them no mind as he continues to look at the enormous and highly immaculate doors that appear to be built for a museum or cathedral. "I'm not gonna lie, though. When I shine my light off of this entrance while you and Séa pose inside these gates right here, this will make some perfect shots." He turns back around to see everyone still looking around. "You still down, Séa...Maria?"

"I'm in. Shoot, the last time I checked a magazine, you didn't need the full building anyway to make a perfect angle. Baby, lift me up over this sharp gate," she requests, lifting her hands up high so Levi can grab her.

"Are you sure it doesn't open first?" Roscoe cuts in as he yanks on the gate from many different angles to try and open it. It's still a bit hard to locate any lock due to the darkness even with everyone's cell phone flashlight on.

"Wait, let me get over the gate first...pass me my stuff. Just don't drop it, Roscoe, man, please. This stuff costs more than tuition this semester," Pierre explains, hopping the iron gate carefully in a spot where there are no spearheads, and then, reaching over for Roscoe to hand him the bag and the light. As soon as Pierre gets situated, he turns on the high beams and the entrance lights up even more.

"Gorgeous. Simply the best photos that we'll take all vacation I bet," Séa sighs. The door reflects a golden, metallic color, and there are images carved in them of what looks like people. Levi rushes to lift his overly excited girlfriend over the gate as even he is amazed by how Pierre set the lighting to bounce off the gold which will be Séa's background.

"These doors had to have been lifted," Maria suggests as she lifts her arms up so that Roscoe can ease her over the gate.

"What do you mean lifted? You mean like stolen?"

"Well, either that or they were borrowed...the design I mean. This doesn't look like a cathedral, but these doors sure are mimicking it. Whoever built this place built it with something grand in mind."

"Let's just get these photos, so we can change the tire and get up outta here," Levi says. "All this darkness and shit." He squints while getting paranoid at the same time. "Can't see anything, can't call anybody because there's no signal and my battery is going dead. I tell you what though," he says looking around with his hand on his piece. "This isn't generally what us black folk do. That being stated, let's hurry the hell up."

Roscoe notices Levi's hand on his gun, and because he is very familiar with his close friend, he becomes suspicious and aware of the surroundings as well. "Man, you good?" Roscoe knows that even though Levi is a hot head, he's very tame when it comes to his pistol, therefore, to see him with his hand on it for no visible reason, triggers an alert.

"Yeah, but be on the lookout with me though. I don't know why I followed Sea's ass up on this one, but this doesn't feel right anymore, man. I just want to get back to the ride." He glances back at Pierre. "Pierre, snap it up quick. We gotta go." He stares through the trees despite the fact that he's doing it blindly. "It's just too quiet. I hear better in noise," he says to himself.

"No problem," Pierre responds. "Give me at the max twenty minutes."

"Ten."

"Levi!" Séa complains about him rushing the photoshoot.

"Ten, Séa! We gotta go, so smile, say cheese and shit, and let's go!" he shouts back at her. Roscoe watches the intensity in Levi's face, so he slowly pulls his knife and keeps on guard. The trees surround the building like a black sheet while the light that shines on from Pierre's stand makes it nearly impossible to see into the trees at all. This is what bothers Roscoe the most of all, so he's depending on his ears only to hear anything other than what's directly behind him with the photoshoot.

Maria, who hasn't totally abandoned all of her uneasiness, leans over to Séa who is busy leaning against the golden door figuring out a pose while Pierre finishes setting up his angle. "Séa, I think Levi may be right on this one. We should just go. We can get pics in the day time at another time."

"In the daytime, Maria," Séa looks over at her annoyed and continues, "this door will look like any other door. You said it yourself, the way it looks right now at night...it's great! Ten minutes and we're out. I want anything that I put on my future comp card to stand out from the rest. Besides that, I said my prayers before I left home. We're good." She continues to memorize the five quick poses that she'll do back to back for Pierre. "These have to be hot poses, Maria, so no smiles. Make it edgy. Smile in your solo shots."

"Ten minutes," she repeats, looking out into the woods and watching Roscoe with his knife at the same time. She also catches Levi with his pistol in hand which leads her to kissing her locket once again before removing it for the photos. She hangs it around the sharp point of the gate, and it shines in the night air. She considers the locket one of love and luck. "Let's get this over with." She takes a deep breath and then moves into the camera's vision.

Pierre starts snapping the camera, and Séa moves around Maria as if she's a prop. Pierre then advises Maria to loosen up and move a bit, so Séa whispers something in her ear that will get her going so the photos won't come out with her looking so stiff.

"Close your eyes and pretend that you are making out with Roscoe. Or better yet, call him. Tell him to turn around and watch," Séa jokes, having the time of her life pretending to be a fashion model.

"Shut up!" she whispers, but the mention of flirting with Roscoe relieves her slightly, putting a bit of pep in her step.

"Hey, Roscoe!" Séa yells, and he turns around, startled by her call until Maria pulls out all stops and shows every single thing that she can possibly give to the camera because the last thing she wants to look like is a stiff in front of the man she wants to attract. She even poses up near the sharp tips of the gate. While Maria does more porn-ish shots, Séa is in full gear for her edge and grunge fashion look. She wants to match the scenery, trying to make a story for her growing portfolio. If she can't make it in modeling one day, then she her plan is to continue to give acting a go.

Six minutes pass and Maria is already ready to go as she eases off to the edge of the gate to request Roscoe's assistance getting over. He does just that, and instead of letting go of his neck as he lifts her over, she holds on, whispering in his ear to chat with her for a second.

"Don't you think I need to put you down first?" Roscoe asks as she straddles her legs around him tightly.

"No, we can talk right here...with me on top of you, if you don't mind. Besides that, I feel better in your arms."

Roscoe glances over at Levi who is already cracking a smile, thinking the whole thing is hilarious as he watches Roscoe hold Maria up from her bosom. Maria is taking being this close and personal with Roscoe all in, not realizing that she's coming on a bit too strong for a man like him.

Roscoe turns back to face her before he takes a spot leaning up against the gate with Maria still in his arms. "So what do you wanna talk about, baby girl?"

"Is that still how you see me?" she smiles, leaning back as if she's offended. "As a baby girl?" She glances up at Séa who is paying her no attention as she wraps up her last poses, and then she zooms in on Roscoe once again.

"How do you want me to see you, birthday girl?"

"I want you to see me as your girl. How's that? Forget the baby girl, and forget me as someone else's girl. Just let me be your girl. Is that possible? Maybe for my birthday, I can unwrap you as my gift?" she asks starting to nibble around his neck.

"Let's ride, man," Roscoe shouts over to Levi, ignoring Maria's overt message to have sex with him, grounding her efforts and leaving her stunned. When he lifts her off of his waist, her feet meet the water soaked ground, and Séa finally looks up in her direction, catching the entire embarrassing episode, shrugs her shoulders, smiles for the last shot, and Pierre shuts it down. Maria checks herself over after being overlooked and under-felt by Roscoe, reminds herself mentally that she is still hot stuff, taps him on his arm and whispers, a bit ashamed because the one thing she wants to do is be able to claim him in front of everyone. She knows how Roscoe is. If he likes a girl, he'll have no problem with publicizing her, but if he just wants to kick it, he'll hide her in the cut. Maria doesn't want the latter location.

"Are you just gonna ignore me like that?" she asks, poking her neck out opening up her hands like she's waiting for him to hand her something. Roscoe grabs Pierre's bag as Pierre lifts Sea over the gate into Levi's arms. When Pierre finally makes it over the gate with his other items, they head off, embarrassed for Maria at this point so much that they don't even say a word. Roscoe starts walking off along with them like he never even got licked down my Maria, and this makes Maria furious. "Roscoe!" she raises her voice, revealing her offence while standing there slightly behind him in complete amazement. She can't believe that Roscoe is leaving her behind after pushing up on her in the house.

Roscoe, on the other hand, is all too cool about the situation. He reaches out for her hand, and at first, she doesn't take it. As he stands there waiting on her, she finally gives in, locking her fingers in between his.

"You play too much," she complains.

"Who says I'm playin', Maria?" he asks with a hint of sarcasm to his voice as he continues to walk, guiding her with his arm so she won't fall over any debris that's in their way.

She yanks his arm, and he stops once again to pay her the attention she desires. "You don't want me? Are you serious? You were just on top of me in the house up there," she points, "and now you act like you're hiding me out. Don't do that to me. I know how you operate, and I'm not with that. I'm twenty years old, Roscoe, come on!" she continues, engulfed in a maximum amount of frustration. "You know I like you, so stop trippin'."

He turns back and watches the crew continue toward the house, and then quickly looks back at Maria to settle her down. "You said you wanted a present. I'll let you unwrap me, and I'll unwrap you." He takes a step back to check out her body, all the while still holding her hand. "Hell yeah I will, but be careful what you ask for." He turns back around to keep walking. "That request doesn't come with anything else, baby. Our relationship will be as thin as the gift wrap."

She snatches her hand away from his. "Excuse me?"

Roscoe finally sits the leather bag down on the ground, and turns to her. "Come here."

"You ain't shit."

"Come here, Maria." Roscoe is aware that he has been making it hard for Maria for quite some time now, long before this trip. He honestly doesn't want to take a friend and make her an enemy, and being that she's about three and a half years younger, her emotions may go in way too deep, far deeper than what Roscoe would even allow himself to fall.

She drags her feet closer to him, but she keeps her head hanging low.

"Hold your head up," he laughs. "You were just about to stick your tongue in my mouth back there at the gate. Don't act like a shy little girl now, ma."

She doesn't respond, but only stares up into his eyes which is when he begins to explain the harshest version of the truth which is that he's only interested in her for her body because she isn't nor hasn't given him much else to pay attention to yet. From day one of her crush, she's bent over backwards trying to get him to notice every nook and cranny when there was no need. Roscoe already saw it.   Therefore, because he truly cares for Maria as a friend, he relays his honesty in the nicest way he can as to not offend too much.

"All jokes aside, and I'm telling you this because you aren't just anyone. You're a friend of mine. I've been seeing you from day one, and, you're fine as hell." He wipes her cheek as a sprinkle of rain falls onto it from the leaves above their heads. "That just won't keep me from another woman who might be just as fine as you. If you were somebody else, I'd have hit that and walked away, but I respect your sexy and our friendship. Now, give me back your hand." He takes it back, and she sulks like a lost puppy. "I just won't hurt you on purpose is all, baby. You ain't never seen me walk around with a trick in public. I'll treat you how you treat yourself. Work on that shit, alright? You show me burger, I give you burger. You show me a better selection, a variety of something other than your fine ass, then I stick around longer – much more to eat on. You feel me?"

"Whatever, Roscoe. I don't know why men have to always use food analogies when it comes to females. Grow up on that!" She pushes ahead of him, but he stops her, grabbing her by her waist. Maria simply stops, but doesn't turn around, intrigued by the way he wants her attention at this very moment. Then he kisses her on her shoulder.

"I see you, birthday girl. I see you," he reassures her which makes her smile again, and he then lets her go, following closely behind in between the trees. Maria, assuming that he's enjoying the view and ignoring what he just told her about offering a better variety, begins to exaggerate her walk for him in an extra special *this exclusive offer* still stands way. Roscoe isn't phased beyond the usual but just laughs it off, choosing to ignore because he's aware that Maria likes him too much for the one night that he would give her if she wasn't a friend. Besides that, his heart is secretly still somewhere else.

By the time they get to the back of the house, Maria remembers something that disturbs every thought of sex on the brain. "Crap, everybody! Crap, crap, crap!" Maria panics, rubbing her neck and chest, spinning around like something is crawling all over her body.

"What, girl, what's wrong?" Séa rushes over to her frantically, immediately checking her hair and neck for spiders and other bugs.

"I lost my locket," she responds panting heavily. "Please, God help me. I lost my locket!" Then, she looks into Séa's eyes with a dreadful amount of tears welling up in her eyes. "It's not on me, Séa! It's not on me!" she cries, tears already streaming down her cheeks. "Mi abuela! Mi abuelita!" she calls for her deceased grandmother.

"Okay, okay, okay...do you remember where you put it?" Séa asks, relieved that it's only a piece of jewelry that can be found. She tries to relax Maria by placing her hands on her shoulders and having her retrace her steps.

"Yeah, I thought I grabbed it, but I guess I didn't. It was hanging on the gate the last time I had it, but I don't know..." Her eyes beam terror back at Séa. "I just can't remember! Roscoe," she continues, "did you see it on me when we left?"

Roscoe shakes his head, but before allowing Roscoe to come to Maria's rescue, Pierre jumps at the chance to go help her find it because the whole way back to the house, he was bothered by the way Maria continued not to notice him at all due to Roscoe's presence. He wants his chance to be alone with her so that he can reveal his true feelings, and this may be his only opportunity for the whole vacation.

"Come on with me. I'll go back down with you to see if we can find it. Cool?"

"Thanks, Pierre. That locket means the world to me, and I can't just leave it here in the middle of nowhere. It was my grandma's, you know, and it brings me blessings."

Levi rolls his eyes, and then he takes a seat on a tree stump. Then, he pulls Séa back toward his lap. "Hey, Pierre, you want this piece?" he asks, handing him his pistol.

"No, man. It's just down the hill. It'll be just a minute. We'll be cool."

"Can't be too safe, man. You see how that snake came outta nowhere on me at the grave, P." Roscoe interjects, sensing that Pierre may truly want some protection with him, just unaware that it won't make him look like a coward, but on the contrary, someone with some sense. This is the reason why Rosoce's next move is handing him his blade. "No sense in taking blind chances with your life. Always be prepared. You got a female to protect." He also is well aware that Pierre has a certain crush on Maria. Roscoe is by no means insecure, and he's already made his feelings crystal clear to Maria. That's why he feels kind of bad for Pierre who is always the butt of many jokes and can't get Maria to pay an ounce of lover attention to him. Therefore, he almost welcomes Pierre the chance to try and hook Maria. Besides, he isn't hooked onto her at all yet.

Pierre takes the knife and nods. "Now that you say that." He turns back to Maria. "Don't worry about it. We'll find it. Wipe your eyes. Come on."

Maria glances up at Roscoe but starts walking side by side with Pierre down the dark and dirty path once again as Pierre holds the knife on his right side. Maria shines her cell phone flash light as they head off, and Roscoe stands there empty of what is considered his armor.

"Pierre is such a punk ass. I don't know when that man is gonna stick his hairy ass chest out like big foot and ask that girl out. She ain't hotter than my lady right here," he states, rubbing Séa's thigh, "so I don't see what the case of nerves is all about."

Roscoe laughs and leans on the back porch of the house. "I don't know, man. He better make good on the opportunity he has right now because she's still throwing herself at me…all the way up here. Did you see that shit?" he asks in reference to Maria licking him on his neck.

"Did I? Man, that girl was about to strip butt naked and do you right on the ground in the mud with her nasty ass. The earth's not even clean yet," he grins, "You know what I mean, man? Muddy ass!"

"Yeah, I almost stopped the shoot. You know she's a virgin right? Don't tell her I said that," Séa chimes in, winking at Roscoe.

"What virgin?" Levi asked, shocked.

"Hell no," Roscoe concurred.

Séa busts out laughing. "I'm lying!"

The three of them continue to joke around as they watch Pierre and Maria disappear into the darkness of the trees.

Chapter Six

"I can't believe this, Pierre. I hope it's not gone because I know it was hanging on one of those spokes things on the top of the gate. Ouch!"

"Sorry, sorry…here…step over here by me. Just walk behind me." He takes her hand and pulls her over behind his body as he is sure to dodge any and everything for the woman whom he wants as his own. "It's there, Maria. We're the only ones out here tonight, and…look."

"Look at what?"

"I can see it from here," he stops her and points to the gate which is about ten feet in front of them. Then he turns back to her to steal the opportunity that he's been waiting on.

"I see it! Thank God! Lemme go run and get it."

Before she can get around him, he gently and nervously touches her stomach to stop her from running. "Wait a minute, Maria."

Maria is caught off guard as the only thing she can think about is her grandmother's silver locket that she gave to her before passing away. Her grandmother prayed over her hands and then placed the locket inside her palms strictly for Maria as a passed blessing. To her grandmother, it was only supposed to be a reminder to follow the blessings in life, but it became more to Maria. She feels like it protects her, but not only that, it makes her feel like she never lost her grandmother being that a piece her precious jewelry hangs on her neck each day since her death.

She glances back at the shining locket, and then back at Pierre. "What's up?"

"Uhm," he stammers, placing the knife into his back pocket before continuing. "Your photos are going to come out really good when I develop the film."

"Thanks. Séa told me that you could work wonders with the camera."

"No! No, no…you're beautiful. I mean, you photograph well, making my job behind the camera easy. I was just wondering if we can make another date for a photoshoot, just you and me sometime, since I've never been able to show you what I can do alone." Pierre's bottom lip quivers like it's a cold, winter night, and after watching Pierre's nerves, Maria is finally sold on his crush on her. She actually thinks he's being quite cute about it, and as she thinks back to Roscoe's noninterest, she decides to remove Pierre's glasses, thinking back on what Séa told her in the bathroom about taking another look at him not just as a good friend or brother type of dude.

"Hold still."

"Wait," he backs up.

"No, it's nothing. Just hold still. I want to see you for who you are, without the glasses, without Levi around or anyone else," she flirts. "I can at least do that, right?" She takes off his glasses. Sure, she's seen him remove his eyewear before, but she's never checked him out like she is now. Séa's right. Pierre has grown into more than just a friend type of guy. "Thanks for walking me back down." Then she gives him a kiss on the lips, and Pierre, whom she thought would freeze up, kisses her back. She enjoys it, and then she steps back, nearly infatuated over the whole encounter. That's when he pulls her back in to him and kisses her again. This time, she wraps her arms around his neck, and totally forgets about Roscoe and the locket for just this moment. Maria believes in kisses being more intimate than anything else, and if she loves a kiss, she considers a love connection.

Pierre slowly backs away from Maria, realizing that it's taking longer than it should to get back. "I guess I can say now that I like you," he says, taking a deep breath with more confidence than he's ever had before. "I would really love to get to know you more than just a friend if you…"

"Sure," Maria cuts him off. "We're already more than friends now," she smiles, blushing and overwhelmed with the thought that she really just kissed Pierre in the mouth. "Oh…here." She hands him back his glasses that she kept hanging from her fingers while they were in a tongue twirl.

"Thanks." He takes them and places them back on his face. Then, she continues to talk as she looks around.

"I wonder what the name of this place is though. It seems so familiar to me still."

"I don't know. When we first got down here to this building, I saw something engraved in the stone that said Doons, but I don't know. I'll check again," he states and then offers, "Let me go get your necklace. Stay put." As he winks at her before turning around, he notices a change in her.

A chill runs down Maria's entire body making her feel like her blood is growing cold. She wants to speak but simply can't when the word Doons comes from his mouth.

"What's the matter? Are you alright?

"Spell it." she orders him as tears well up in her eyes, and she begins to shake. She takes her eyes off of him, suddenly realizing where she is as she examines the surroundings behind her as she turns around to face the houses she just left.

"Spell..."

As soon as she hears him, she cuts him off. "Just spell it!"

"Doons...D.O.O.N.S.," Pierre states, getting really concerned. "What, Maria, what?" He asks, but she won't answer, so he just decides to run and grab the necklace, but suddenly there's a shuffle in the bushes behind him. He feels the knife being yanked from his pants pocket, and when he twists to feel for it, he hears a deathly scream come from Maria who has now turned back around to face pure horror standing behind Pierre.

Immediately, he turns back for her, and while his eyes become perplexed inside her terrified gaze, he is grabbed from behind at his throat. When he fights to get free, his flesh splits in two as he feels the plunging of a knife penetrating his back and side repeatedly. Maria muffles her screams incidentally with her hands while she watches Pierre's entire body being flung back and forth by the knife being repeatedly shoved into his body, ripping his insides apart. He reaches out for Maria's help as he struggles for his life as the blood begins to run through his light yellow shirt, but Maria only stands in shock staring, not back at Pierre, but at the beast of a man behind him, cutting and stabbing her friend over and over again. The killer looks directly into Maria's eyes as the midsection of Pierre's back is being shredded to limp pieces.

"Pierre, no!" she screams, finally pulling his arm, but the more she pulls him, the harder the man twists the knife into Pierre's side. The killer stares her in the face, as he chuckles like a maniac at his kill. Pierre struggles to gain composure enough to strike backwards, but the more he swings backwards, the more energy he loses until he falls to the ground, leaving nothing but the wind between himself and Maria.

Maria watches the body of Pierre drop to the ground, and her screams come to a pause when she looks back up to see the killer staring her back in the face. He stands there, watching Maria back away while her composure is shaken by fear causing her to nearly trip up on the ground. The killer takes one step forward, stepping over the bloody Pierre on the ground, and as he does, Maria strips her throat of all power and might as she yells for help standing only a few feet from the man who just sent Pierre to the ground. She realizes that she is next, but in seconds, the man who just tore through Pierre's body like it was grocery store meat, glances up to notice people running toward her. He then leaps into the trees.

"Maria! Maria!" Séa cries as Roscoe and Levi run ahead of her only to find Maria backing up with her hands out to the sides like she's feeling for walls when there are none. Her left hand grips her cell phone tightly, and her right hand is flexed and appears strained as she screams at the top of her lungs. As they run around her, they find Pierre shivering on the wet, muddy ground face down, his eyes staring straight ahead of him with Roscoe's knife shoved inside his back. Pierre's glasses are knocked off his face, and his body is arched as he lies there in shock, struggling to keep himself alive.

"Pierre!" Levi falls down to the ground, staring his cousin directly in the face as he desperately tries to cling to life. "Pierre, what happened to you? What happened, man," he yells, his eyes constantly looking back and forth at the knife that's sticking out of his back and back into his cousin's tearing eyes. "Take that shit out of his back! Pierre!" he yells again. "You're not gonna die, man, come on and get up," he says, pulling at his upper body. "Keep breathing, keep on breathing!" Then, Levi stands up hysterical, drawing his pistol looking for someone to shoot. The gun lands on Maria. "Who the fuck did this? Was it you?"

"No! It wasn't me. It was some man! Some man! It's the Doons! This is the Doons!" she hollers as Séa jumps in front of her, protecting her from Levi who looks like he's about to lose his mind. No one pays attention to Maria hollering the name of the place because they're so used to her speaking Spanish, so they assume she is saying something in her native tongue.

"Why would she do this, Levi! Leave her alone," Séa pleads, "Please, leave her alone!"

"I said take that fuckin' knife from his back!" Levi shifts his attention to Roscoe, continuing to lash out in anger at the sight of his cousin on the ground dying. Then, he reaches for the knife that juts out of Pierre's back himself, but Roscoe blocks him which is a mistake. "Man, I will blow your fuckin' mind from your skull if you touch me again," he warns, placing the gun against Roscoe's cheek. Roscoe throws his hands up from leaning over Pierre's back to answer Levi's gun to his cheek with a solid and sure statement.

"Levi, we can't remove the knife man because it's gonna make another cut that might kill him," he stresses, attempting to remain calm while the gun is on his face, but calmness is such a fabrication because his lips are curled and his teeth are grinding up against one another as he speaks. "We gotta get him to the hospital just like he is and fast, but we gotta move. Taking the knife out is gonna make things worse. Trust me, man. I know." Roscoe then takes a deep breath, and speaks slower, enunciating every word from his mouth. His head is tilted, and only his eyes cut to the side to zoom in on

Levi's finger on the trigger. "Now take the mother fuckin' gun from my face, Levi, if you're not gonna blow a hole in my head. Then you can think about how you're gonna move this man your damn self."

Maria is still screaming at an unbearably high pitch and shaking so badly that she can barely stand up. Séa covers her mouth in horror at the sight of Pierre in convulsions while blood seeps from his mouth. Then she spins around to face the woods, panicked by the plain facts -there's a killer among them, and he just tried to stab Pierre to death.

"Pick him up," Séa quietly states, and as she continues to strain her eyes to see further into the woods, she elevates her voice. "Pick him up, now! We gotta get outta here," she screams at Levi as he backs away from Roscoe's face with the gun. "Hurry!" She glares at Levi like she wants to shoot everyone if they don't make the right moves, and then she snatches the gun from his hand. "Gimme the gun, Levi. Give me the fuckin' gun, dammit!" She quickly points the gun toward the woods, ready to fire at the first human moving that she doesn't recognize. Her heart beats rapidly through her chest, almost to the point of feeling like it will explode. Séa's a small young lady, but she's ready to defend herself at all costs. If anyone will shoot to kill, Levi knows that it's her, therefore, he plays the odds that she will more than likely hit the necessary target while he does something he has no choice but to do – relieve himself of the firearm and help Roscoe pick up a weak and bleeding to death Pierre off the muddy ground.

"Go! Go!" Roscoe yells at Levi, ordering him to get himself together so they can lift Pierre to safety because he knows that fast movement is the only chance Pierre has to stay alive due to blood loss and injuries. Roscoe's knife isn't meant to slice. The jagged edges are meant to mutilate, and as he stares down at the protruding weapon rising from Pierre's back, he begins to mourn silently for what he can almost foresee - death. He looks up at Maria. "Maria, we need you to shut the hell up and lead us back to the house. Can you do that? Shut the hell up and walk back to the house." Roscoe is pissed. Before sadness, he's always been one to resort to anger. He did the same thing when Justynn was killed.

Finally, they lift Pierre on the count of three while Maria, although shivering like it's twenty degrees outside, starts on her way toward the house, but then she stops in her tracks.

"What the fuck did you stop for? Go! Damn!" Levi shouts.

"This is the Doons! This is the same place! There was a slaughter here," she weeps, "years ago." She quiets down. "I have been here before. I was four years old…"

Roscoe butts in, hearing enough of the story at the word slaughter. "That's enough of that slaughter shit because we're not dying. We'll kill his ass, and fuck a Doons. Now, if you see anything, Maria, start that screaming shit again. Séa, you aim behind us. If you see anything come within two arms lengths of us, blast. Hold on to the back of my pants to guide your way. Levi," he states, under full knowledge that he has the most bearings about himself right now due to Levi having to watch and carry his dying cousin. No matter how much they fight, they love each other. Levi is trying his best to hold back the tears as Pierre's upper body is hooked inside his arms. "Levi, walk as fast as you can, so we can wrap him up at the truck." He pauses to look around. "When we see this mother fucker, we're gonna kill him." Levi looks back at Roscoe, and he knows at this point that they are truly a team again, at least for this mission. Instead of trying to speak, he turns back around to follow Maria, keeping his eyes peeled while awaiting the right moment to relieve himself of his inner pain, either on the killer or alone. Unfortunately, right now, his eyes are planted on Maria's back, and as he follows behind, his anger builds due to his doubt of her innocence because he needs someone to blame that's tangible. At this point, it's her. In the meantime, Séa is led by Roscoe, gun drawn and ready for action.

The wind picks up on the trek back, and each time a branch moves, Séa swings the pistol in that direction. She can't get what Maria said out of the back of her head. Just the thought of there having been a slaughter here takes her mental state into one that is survival mode, so she steadily picks up her feet, remaining as close as she can to Roscoe. The house comes into full view, but instead of going inside, Maria leads them to the side of the house, straight back to the SUV as she shakes violently and overwhelmed with shock, forgetting the bags and camera equipment they left on the back porch.

"Let's go, let's go! Séa, run and get the back door open," Levi orders, feeling more comfortable in the open area in front of the house. Pierre's vitals appear like they have plummeted to their worst yet, and Maria is just standing there watching, her knees about to give out as she feels her chest, missing her necklace and grandmother's locket.

"Abuelita, por favor..." she continues to whisper in broken breaths as she looks from side to side, afraid of the wind's movement. The make-up that she placed on her face for the photoshoot is all gone as a result of her tears, and the only thing left disguising her natural beauty is the horror that seeps through her eyes. "I'm gonna die...abuelita...Es el Doons, abuelita."

Séa, Levi and Roscoe all jump in the Expedition, oblivious of Maria's silent rage only three feet away from the vehicle. As Levi is pulling off, Séa notices that Maria didn't get inside. Puzzled, she rushes out of the vehicle as Levi beeps the horn for her to snap out of it. As the horn blows and Levi yells at the top of his lungs for her to get in, Séa begins to shake her violently.

"Wake up and let's go! Get in before we leave!"

Her grandmother's name continues to stream from her mouth with the doomsday babble that Séa isn't trying to believe in because all she's focusing on is the prayer she prayed to herself on the way to the SUV for God to get them out of harms way. Because Maria won't stop, she slaps the side of her face so hard that Maria comes to her senses only for a moment. Then her light brown eyes stare back into Séa's eyes, only to be interrupted by Roscoe who jumps from the car, ready to toss her inside with the understanding that she's been traumatized beyond understanding as she watched Pierre get attacked. Before he picks her up, he stands mesmerized looking at her back.

"What?" Séa asks bewildered until she follows the imaginary path drawn by Roscoe's eyes. She walks around to the back of Maria as she stands there mumbling the mumblings similar to that of someone insane or so it seems. As Séa turns toward the direction in which Roscoe is staring, there's a arrow shot and jammed directly into the middle of her back.

Maria's mumblings don't sound so out of place anymore as Séa backs up only to release the worst scream Levi's ever heard. The night seems to stand still, becoming extremely quiet as if its only course of action is to decipher Séa's screams while Roscoe stands stunned with Maria. Levi rushes from the truck to grab Séa in his arms believing she's in danger, but when he sees the arrow stuck in Maria's back, he turns his girlfriend away. She resists him, and being consumed with emotional pain at the sight of her best friend attacked from afar by some madman, she lashes out.

"I'm gonna kill you whoever did this!" she screams continuously, but Levi continues to hold her as he covers her mouth to no avail. "Please, Levi," she cries, "Please let me go so I can find him and kill him, please...oh God," she weeps, falling to the ground. Her short hair scrapes the mud as her head falls forward into her hands. Levi remains quiet, seemingly numb, but the quivering of his lips tells the story of a man on the edge. He lifts Séa from the ground, takes her to the truck and places her in the passenger's seat before he makes his way to the back of Maria with Roscoe.

"Can we pull this one out?" Levi asks, choking back his emotion. As Levi struggles within himself, Roscoe is not only doing the same, but he notices something shiny hanging from the sharp point of the arrow that's sticking in her back. He reaches for it, touching it with his index and middle fingers.

"What the hell?" Levi squints, leaning in to only find the locket that Maria's grandmother left her, the one that she adores so much, tied around the weapon. His eyes follow the locket onto the linked chain, and as his eyes make their way up the necklace link by link, the conclusion of the trail is inside Maria's body. Levi immediately looks up at Roscoe, and Roscoe quickly mutes him by lifting his hand. Levi's tongue grows weighted as he sorrowfully looks at the back of Maria's head while she continues to stammer in a language they can't understand.

Roscoe quickly finishes ripping her tank top where the arrow already struck in order to expose the sophisticated network of her spinal column from beneath her skin. Then, he leans over very closely to Maria's ear, causing her to become startled. She even jerks away when he comes near her ear as if she doesn't know he's been standing there the whole time.

"I need to feel up your back to see if I can pull this bow out. I mean, I don't know if I can, but I'm just gonna use some common sense, so let's lean over just a little maybe," he states, but as soon as he touches her to force her over, she releases agony. "Okay, okay! Shhh..," he silences her, holding her shoulders tightly.

He looks back at Levi. "We got no choice, man. I don't think it's that deep. On three, pull it out."

On the count, Levi eyes the arrow and pulls. It comes out, and he drops it on the ground, along with the Maria's necklace and locket. Maria starts to turn around, after screaming from the pain of something coming out of her body, and he places his foot on top of the locket, concealing it from his already distraught and injured friend.

"Can you walk?" Roscoe asks while Levi draws his gun.

Maria, who now appears less like a young lady but more like a little girl who just wants to crawl inside her mother's arms, shakes her head. She then looks at Roscoe. "It doesn't matter though. He's here, Roscoe. Didn't you listen to me?"

Roscoe ignores her. "Try...and if you can walk, we can sit you down. Please, Maria, or I'm gonna have to throw you in the SUV," Roscoe explains, getting frustrated as Séa approaches her friend after removing herself once again from the SUV, more confident for her after seeing the arrow removed safely from her back.

"Come on, Maria," Séa reaches out to coerce her into moving quickly. "We're gonna be okay. Just get in." Then, she stops when she catches a glimpse of Maria's locket, slightly uncovered at the feet of Levi. "What?" She leans over, but Levi silences her, motioning his eyes toward the SUV. Séa doesn't even pretend she knows what he's saying, so she grabs it, noticing blood and the connection to the arrow. As she pulls the necklace and watches it unravel from the arrow, a stunned Séa drops it back onto the ground and begins to pull Maria toward the truck until the truck suddenly drops.

Maria stops limping forward immediately. "Stop. Everyone stop!" The SUV drops once more, and Séa, Levi and Roscoe are all startled together as they jump inwards, crowding in toward Maria who seems to know more than what they all do about what's going on. "Stop running!" She then quiets. "He's here." She turns to see all of them, and then looks out at everything else around her. "We're inside the Gates of Doons." Her breath pants like a person near death. "I remember. My great uncle was murdered here. He was a homeless man, mentally ill but ready to fit in to society. Before he got out, the killer..." she pauses, "of the Doons...he killed him." Maria's eyes begin to blink away the tears that build in her eyes as she looks toward the bottom of the SUV. "That building back there is the mental facility. It's shut down, but he killed a bunch of people overnight when there were no visitors, and no one to see. Some of the people there always made noise all night long, so a scream wasn't out of the norm, I heard. He went from room to room. They shut the place down, and it's been abandoned ever since because they never found the killer because he had no address and no family, no nothing." she says trembling. "I would listen to grandma tell the story to her friends sometimes because she never could get over it." She takes her eyes off of the ground beneath the SUV and plants them on Séa. "For all we know, he's still here...alive," she continues solemnly. "I came to visit my uncle at the facility with my mom at four years old. She told me my uncle was dead when I turned five." She stares forward. "The killer of the Doons – he's a psychopath. According to authorities, he killed when he was only seven. My mom told me about it when I got older - that he stalks people, watches them, learns them...and has a history of killing them..."

The rental falls again, breaking Maria's story before she finishes. "What the fuck?" Levi exclaims as his rental falls lower on the other side and then at the very back. They all glance at one another for an answer as to why this is happening, but it becomes obvious that it wasn't just the other tire going flat. Someone must be flattening the tires.

Without hesitation, Roscoe snatches the bloody arrow from off the ground, causing Maria to see her grandmother's locket. She grabs the arrow in a flurry of emotion and won't let go as Roscoe starts around the SUV to defend the crew.

"Give me my locket!" Maria pulls hard at the arrow, but Roscoe angrily and forcefully strips it from her hand. "Abuelita! Abuelita!" she screams for her deceased kin as Séa starts to pull her further away from the SUV that has collapsed before their very eyes. Séa watches both Roscoe and Levi run to the other side of the truck, and things grow silent, a bit too silent, and her paranoia forces her to spin around in circles to check every inch of area around her and the hysterical Maria.

When Séa faces the SUV again, she drops to the ground to check for feet underneath the vehicle, but when she sees none, she hauls Maria to the truck and helps her inside as Maria holds on tightly to her shoulder. There's a heel on the floor of the truck, one that looks to be six inches that she can use like a blade. Séa grabs it

106

and jumps back out of the truck while locking the fatally wounded Pierre and Maria inside.

"Levi!" she yells, but gets no answer. At that, she turns to look in the window at Pierre, but more so the knife in his back, contemplating whether or not she should remove it for her own protection.

Chapter Seven

Roscoe and Levi hear disturbing groans coming from a small distance away in the trees. The groans gain volume, and every time they hear it, it sounds like it's coming from all directions because they can't pinpoint it. When they walked around the SUV only seconds ago, they were startled at the fact that not one but two of the tires were sliced completely open, making their worst fears come true – being stranded. They now have to get away on foot which means lifting Pierre to safety. That in itself would prove to be a struggle as things are far worse after Maria is shot in the back. The only option now is to kill or be killed.

In the background, they hear Séa calling, screaming the words *where are you*, but they don't answer due to their concentration completely stolen by the thought of getting out alive. At this moment, they're cornered in a vastly open area with nowhere to go fast. As the groans continue, they start to hear chuckles mix in with them, but there's nothing funny.

"Don't yell back at his giggling ass," Roscoe warns Levi because he knows how hot headed he can get. "Let's fish him out. Hook that bitch and drag him to us, and let him laugh then. I know what his ass is laughing at…it's because he's trying to fish us," Roscoe states, looking around carefully at the immediate area. His normally clean attire is caught up in mud from his shoes to his pant leg cuffs, but he isn't concerned. His concerns lie in getting out alive. "We need to get back to Pierre, Maria and Séa. We're gonna use those clothes to pull Pierre up out of here, make them into a sort of sheet and drag him out, one person on each end. Forget those tires and that truck. Let's go."

"That's a bet." Levi looks around in front of himself once more, but when they turn around to head back to Séa, there's an image standing forty paces in front of them, his head cocked to the side and draped in black. Although Levi and Roscoe have never seen the killer, they know it's him. His stance is one that's leaned forward and he has absolutely no motion. The wind blows leaves and small branches in between them on the road as the adrenaline rushes through their bodies, never having looked a serial killer in the face before. Levi grips his gun tightly as he and Roscoe stand there locking eyes with the killer. As they stand there, the image standing before them turns around slowly. He only stops when his back is turned to them. After taking a deep breath, he begins to proceed forward at a marcher's pace on one single mission only - to kill the ones left defenseless Séa and Maria.

"Séa!" Levi raises his gun and fires blindly in a panic for his future fiancée's life, but misses as he watches the culprit pick up his pace and run straight in the direction that he fears most.

**

"Levi! Come back!" screams Séa as she walks in front of the SUV. She looks back at Maria who is now sitting up, rocking back and forth totally bombarded by the chills because she's overtaken by bad nerves. Maria's eyes are still wide open, however, at her best friend who has a high heel in her hand to use as a weapon in case she needs it. Just as Maria turns her head to the side slightly, she becomes startled by a fast motion in the darkness, but when she turns back to face Séa, she leaps onto the windshield, hands plastered against it in a common criminal's stance. The SUV lights automatically shut off as she bangs as hard as she can to alert her to the threat that stands behind.

Séa quickly turns to face her, hearing the bang against the windshield. She watches Maria's mouth wide open and screaming with tears streaming down her face. Séa stops moving as she feels the warmth of deep breaths rubbing against the back of her neck, but she dares not look back as she spots Levi and Roscoe running directly her way. Knowing that she'll be overpowered from behind, she tries to make a run for it but is snatched backwards by her neck and pulled up off the ground in a head lock, feet dangling as she kicks and swings her high heel behind her in hopes to strike a target. Levi and Roscoe finally reach the SUV only to agonizingly watch Séa being dragged backwards in the direction of the beat up shack, unable to speak due to the arm around her neck. He yanks Séa's heel she's swinging from her hand, and Séa buckles in fear, beginning to struggle even harder for her life as she feels herself losing more of her capacity to breathe. Then, he raises the high heel into the air as he leans his head forward into the area of her eyebrow. Then, he loosens his grip on her neck just enough so that she can get enough air into her system to stay alive. Rubbing the high heel against her curly hair, he groans and pretends to adore her scent. His eyes dig into the man whom he knows as her boyfriend, and he can almost taste the rage boiling over inside of Levi while he holds the useless gun in his hand.

"Shoot your gun," the man whispers in a tone that carries all the way over into Levi's ears. The voice is deep and evil enough to cut all the way through to the depths of hell. His breath reeks off bile and in the middle of his terror-filled reign, he leans further in with his eyes focused on Levi and slides his tongue into the corner of Séa's mouth.

"God!" Séa cries as the hooded man opens his mouth to portray the shock that he has left the two men in that stand before him. Then, he starts to hit Séa in the head with his knuckles every time he takes a step closer to the house. When Levi finally takes a step forward to attack, he raises the heel again and penetrates Séa's thigh.

Séa screams with the inability to contain her screeches as a result of the pain. Both her legs elevate from the ground once more, but this time by her own power as she makes the attempt to drop to the ground from the agony. He stops her by holding her at standing height. She tries to reach her thigh for comfort, but he rips the pointed heel out of her leg, throwing it directly into the windshield at a gazing Maria who melts into tears, her screams muffled because she's on the inside.

"Séa!" a helpless Levi cries as he lifts the gun in surrender, allowing it to hang from his fingers in efforts to bargain with the man who could potentially kill the woman he loves. His voice cracks as he begs, "Take me, man, take me. Let her go."

Her thigh is now oozing blood and erupting in so much pain that she can't fight him anymore. As he starts to give her knuckle blows to the head again, he groans like he's gaining strength from her pain and watching them beg for his mercy. When Levi feels that his request is going unanswered, he aims his gun once again, desiring to shoot but knowing that he wouldn't be able to live more than five seconds more if he shoots Séa.

"Put her the fuck down!" Levi yells, but then Roscoe starts to walk toward the attacker, seeing that all the perpetrator has is his fist to fight with now that he's thrown the high heel, but when a long blade is pulled and pressed against Séa's throat, plans change. Roscoe becomes stagnated. Séa's breathing quickly stops as she grows tense with her eyes planted on Roscoe and looking back at an infuriated Levi who is ready to kill. Before their very eyes, the killer tosses her forward and yanks her weakened body right back by the neck like he's tossing a yo-yo. As he holds the back of her neck inside the grip of his hand, he slices it gently from one side to the other, only making a small cut, gaining power from the helplessness that has overcome the young group of travelers.

Maria, who watches from the SUV, bangs the window, tolerating the pain that shoots through her side every time she moves her upper body, before she flicks on the lights of the SUV again only to see what she didn't see happening so vividly - Séa's blood trickle down the killer's knife. "Séa!" she screams in terror as she finds the courage to reach for the door's handle and unlock the SUV to come out. As she steps forward, she falls down to the ground, unaware of just how badly her back is injured.

"Get back in the truck!" Levi yells, only hearing, not seeing, Maria fall to the ground. Levi hasn't taken his eyes off of Séa one time, and with each step the killer take toward the house, Levi inches forward as well, waiting on a chance to shoot and kill. He's waiting on the one wrong move that he believes the killer will make so that he can take his shot and Séa can run, but it's too late. As Levi's palms are sweating and burning from holding the pistol so tightly, the killer lifts Séa's entire midsection up to cover his upper body when he reaches the porch. With each step, Levi's hand is closer to pulling the trigger as Roscoe is also itching to pounce. Just then, the SUV's lights go out again, startling everyone, and in a split second of darkness, Séa disappears with the killer into the house, the door shutting behind them.

"Séa!" Levi runs up to the door, and then he kicks it twice, weakening the lock. Roscoe then makes it up to the door, lifts two fingers as a countdown to Levi, and then, he finishes the job. The door is kicked completely open, but when they glance inside – no one.

"Roscoe!" Maria calls from the ground, and he turns back to help her up while Levi handles himself with the gun.

114

"Go ahead, man, I got this. Hurry up!" He continues to glance around. "Séa!" he calls, but gets no response. "Séa!" He looks back to see that Roscoe is already tending to Maria and feels pressed to find out the status of his cousin Pierre, so he makes the difficult decision to check on him quickly before going to get Séa because at this point, he doesn't know where she is.

Jumping inside the truck, he places his hand on Pierre when he notices that his chest isn't going up and down. "Roscoe!" he cries. "Hey, Coe, come here, man." Levi falls against the frame of the truck as he stares at the body of his cousin just lying there lifeless with the knife coming from his back draped in clothes to try and clot it up.

After helping Maria safely back into the SUV, Roscoe locks all the doors behind him as he climbs inside, rushing to get to Pierre. He leans across the seat to place his fingers on Pierre's neck and holds it there for three seconds. He gets nothing. Hesitantly glancing over at Levi who is breathing sporadically at the thought of his cousin dying, he feels again for a pulse a Pierre's throat, but still gets nothing.

"Levi, we gotta take the knife out and turn him over."

"He's dead?" Levi asks, not really wanting to know the answer.

"Just let me pull the knife out and do CPR," Roscoe continues, a tear finally falling from his face while he struggles to stay focused on his training.

"Man, I asked you a question!" Levi punches the seat awaiting a straight answer from Roscoe as he looks at the motionless fingertips of Pierre.

"Man, yes!" Roscoe hollers, taking his fist and ramming it into the window. "Yes, he's fuckin' dead!"

At the sound of those words, Levi falls over atop his cousin, kisses him on the cheek while Pierre's eyes stare blindly straight ahead, unwraps the bloody clothes from around the knife that's stuck in Pierre's back, and then pulls it out. There's no emotion showing anymore in Levi's face as he hands the knife to Roscoe. "It's time to go kill this mother fucker."

"Wrap me up, Roscoe." Maria looks up hopeful that they won't leave her behind with a deceased Pierre. "I need to help you find her. I can do it. Just wrap me up." She looks at Pierre one last time and blinks her tears back. "I can't...I can't stay in here. I feel like it was my fault."

"Fix her up real quick, Coe, and let's go get Séa," he says wiping the tears from his eyes, holding in his anger for the one he wants to take it out on most. "Find whatever we can use in this rental. We need to break off whatever we can for you to use, Maria, so you can fight back."

"Where's that arrow?" she asks.

"I dropped it outside." Roscoe says, hurrying to dump more shirts from the duffle and tie them together to wrap them tightly around her body. "Here tie these together tightly."

"Look in my purse. Just dump it. I have pain meds in there. Give me four. I'll put four more in my pocket."

"Cool," Roscoe answers. "Don't look at him, Levi. He's gone. God has him now. He was a good kid. We'll be back to get him and take him out of here. Levi, man," he speaks louder and more commanding as he halts his patching of Maria. "We're getting out of here, and Pierre is, too. This ain't a fuckin' movie." He finishes wrapping Maria. "Fuck the killer of the Doons. Our asses are the killers of the fuckin' Doons tonight. Let's go kill this mother fucker for Pierre and get Séa."

Maria swallows four pain killers, and instead of taking only four more in her pocket, she takes the whole bottle along with her. Then, she finds the cooler and unloads one of Roscoe's protein drinks to coat her stomach from the amount of meds that will numb the pain. She then leans in and gives Pierre her last tearful kiss on the cheek and closes his eyes.

As soon as their feet hit the mud, Maria immediately spots her locket that apparently dropped on the ground when Roscoe approached the killer with the arrow. She walks through the lessening pain to get it off of the ground and picks up the arrow that was once jabbed through her skin. She reaches back and presses down on the wound, finding that it is still so tender at the touch. Wanting the meds to kick in faster so that she won't slow things up when finding Séa, she reaches in her bottle to take more, but Levi stops her.

"Don't go overdosing. We need you to walk and run. Let the medicine kick in." He walks ahead of her on a mission, and Roscoe grabs her hand, pulling her along.

Without hesitation, Levi walks into the house ready to shoot, and Roscoe follows behind, leaving Maria at the closed front door. They scan the room, and when they prepare to go upstairs, Maria walks over to the back door instead after noticing something of Séa's. Then, she peers out of the back window. It's one of the earrings Séa was wearing before she was taken.

"Levi! Roscoe!" She points, continuously hitting the window with her finger. "I think they went back there."

They both run down the stairs. "How do you figure?" Levi asks.

"Her earring is on the floor. She was wearing both of them just now outside and," she says, growing fatigued from standing so she leans up against the railing, hooking her grandmother's necklace back around her neck, "Now it's here at the doorway."

"Good eyes. Let's go." Levi states as Roscoe follows suit.

"Get on my back. As I'm walking, you keep your head turning. Got it?" Roscoe asks.

"Uhm hmm," she agrees. "Thanks, I'll be fine. Just give me a minute. I think it's just the meds."

"You just have to tighten it up and endure it to make it out of here alive. We're wasting time. Hop on." He leans over and gets down on one knee waiting.

"She's not dead."

Levi and Roscoe turn back to stare at her, growing increasingly annoyed because they have to slow down for her sake. This results in an agitated Levi verbally attacking her after the comment.

"How do you know, Maria, since you've known more about this fucked up place than us in the damn last ass hour?" Levi responds frustrated. "It's some damn amazing shit," he scowls, "that your mentally suppressed ass couldn't recall that we pulled up in a damn slaughter house at the damn gate, but now your ass is foretelling shit and naming names like it's damn story time!"

She shouts back, "Well, I didn't know, alright! I told you that I felt like I'd been here before. Don't blame me!"

"That just ain't some shit you just forget, Maria. You're the only one that's originally from this place, so you know the most."

"I thought it was over! I knew about what happened when I was only a kid, okay! A fucking kid!"

"Chill. Just," Roscoe interjects, grabbing her hand. "How do you know that this killer isn't dead? Do you know something more about this dude?"

"Like I told you, the story was that he likes to play games. It was said that he probably died or something, but nobody really found him to make an arrest nor did they find his body anywhere either. When the authorities were called to the slaughter, the papers said that there was no one found that just dropped dead at that place," she states, looking out the window. "All the deaths led to the other deaths which means that he studied the people he was gonna kill, and made it like a domino effect, ripping their throats out if they liked to laugh, busting their teeth out if they liked to talk. They said he killed one whole hall of patients in one night before bedtime because he knew who would be where when and what triggered them, at least that was the story coming from staff and some patients who survived I was told. Upon identification of the bodies, his was the only one missing." She touches her locket. "It's the same thing he did with me and Pierre when I left my necklace. He knew I would come for it. He knew my trigger. If I wouldn't have left it..." she starts to cry, and Roscoe tries to comfort her, but she wipes her eyes quickly. "Let's just go. Just know that she's alive because he wants to trap us, too. Let's just not die, okay?" She stares at them both, despite their frustration. "We stick together, okay?"

"His ass is gonna trap us alright, but the results won't be like he thinks." Levi courageously walks out the door. Roscoe loads Maria onto his back, and they walk back down the path in jet black darkness and on high alert as they approach the main building of the Doons.

As they reach the gate, they begin searching for a better entrance in the complete darkness. All of their cell phones are now dead, and Levi's got lost on during the chase, therefore, the light that they would have had is nonexistent. As Levi feels his way around one side of the gate and Roscoe around the other, they finally give up and decide to go over one at a time. Levi is the first to hop over.

"Come on, Maria. Lift your legs high so you won't cut your legs on these sharp tips."

"I'm gonna lift them as high as possible, Levi. Just don't drop me."

"I won't." He nods to Roscoe, and he lifts her up underneath her arms as they manage to get her over with little pain. Next, Roscoe goes over the gate in the same area where Levi got over – where there's a break in the sharp points of the fence. About three of the tips are broken completely off at the base making it easier for anyone able bodied to cross.

All of them face the door and notice the small, corroded sign that they missed when they were here before which says Doons Mental Facility. As they walk closer, up the steps to the heavy and over sized golden doors, they do something that no one did the first time they came up here – pull down on the door handle. The door opens, and immediately, the smell of rot that had been contained inside the stone walls greets them without resistance. Slithering maggots fall from the door directly in front of them, startling Maria, causing her to fall backwards into Roscoe as some reach her shirt and hair. She knocks them off and watches them crawl on the ground all around their feet. Normally, she would have screamed, however, the atmosphere is filled with not only the moist air they came here with, but it's also overflowing with death. It's this deathly overcast that seals her lips from making any unnecessary noise.

Levi takes the first step inside the doorway, turning back to confirm that Roscoe still has his back. With his left arm guarding Maria who is now taking her first steps inside behind him, he lifts his pistol but realizes that he can barely see anything. As Roscoe moves in behind them, he finds that there is no way for the door to remain open, so he allows it to close, losing the light that was given outside by the full moon. The only source of light that reaches inside is from the windows that tower up to the high ceiling, allowing the three friends to see the huge staircase that goes up for three floors. Finally, someone speaks.

"Yeah...this is where my late uncle lived. I remember this because there used to be a big center desk or something right there, directly in front of us. From what mom said, the news report told of the blood streaming like a river coming down the stairs," she continues walking behind Levi as she squeezes the arrow in her hand until they hear Séa's loud scream coming from beyond the walls.

"Séa!" Levi calls frantically, but all he gets is an echo. He spins around, staring everywhere as he hears her voice bouncing off of the walls as if he's standing in a cave in the middle of nowhere. He yells again, out of breath, like he just finished running a marathon. His breathing is gaining speed and depth as he continues to call her again. "Séa! Séa, baby, left or right? Left or right Séa from the entrance, baby, left or right? Where do I find you?"

All three of them listen, holding onto the edge of their own lives as they wait for answer when a loud, deep scrape rips slowly across the walls around them.

"What the hell is that?" Levi asks, searching in vain with his gun pointing at every angle.

"Man, fuck that noise," Roscoe responds confidently to Levi after suffocating any ounce of fear that crept up. He regains his composure, and continues, "Nobody's behind me, and if there was, shoot him. He bleeds just like us." Then he demands, "Séa, scream! Scream loud so we can come get you and get up out of here!"

There's no response to Roscoe's demand, therefore, they continue to walk, every thirty seconds listening to a scrape on the walls. It's so terrifying that it weakens Maria's stomach to the point that she vomits. When she regurgitates, severe aches burn her throat that cause her to moan in agony while the inflamed muscles in her back contract to the point of despair. Her projectile vomit goes directly in the path of Levi who stands in front of her, barely missing his clothing.

"Mi Dios! My back!" she strains in the difficult attempt to ease her pain and remain quiet.

Roscoe moves quickly to help hold her back in a comfortable position while she recovers. "Don't worry," he convinces her, pulling her up so that she can stare him directly in his face. "Now isn't the time to get scared and take your body through more changes. Didn't your mom ever tell you not to come back home unless you win the fight?" He asks trying his best to see in the dark, but the fact of the matter still stands that it's nearly impossible.

"Yeah," she moans.

"Well, this is that time. I'm not running from this mother fucker, Maria," he informs her as if she doesn't already know. Roscoe has never been a coward nor fearful of much of anything. Cautious, but never fearful. She knows that if he fights, he fights to keep his opponent down, and if he has to die, then his plan is to die fighting to live. Therefore, she's well aware that she's the weakest link. "If anything, Maria, you have to throw the killing dagger. Got it?"

"I know. I'll be ready," she agrees, taking a deep breath to remain composed, but she also recalls the story of the killer of the Doons – how he watches and learns people – which is obviously a part of his psychological impairments, almost like a stalker. "What if he's watching us, Roscoe?" she asks shakily and quietly. "Calculating how he can kill us all?"

"Well then he just heard what the hell I said. Are you cool now because we have to move?"

"Yeah, I can make it." Her grandmother's locket hangs from the necklace around her neck, and she strokes the crucifix embedded into the front of it as a design. She remembers the words of her grandmother who always told her to move through the good or bad times. This is the worst time of her life, but she gains strength from knowing that if her grandmother was still on earth, she wouldn't want her to give up and run. Some things, she knows she has to attack.

"Man, I'm gonna have to leave you and Maria," Levi says, irritated, angry and just wanting to find his girlfriend and leave. "She's holding us up, Roscoe, and I need to find Séa. With Maria limping and throwing all up..." he pauses, glancing down at the floor and then back up at Roscoe. "Look, man, you stay here with Maria, and I have to go and..."

Roscoe moves Maria to the side so that he can move closer to Levi's face in order to keep the tone down. "What the hell you mean *you're walking alone to find Séa*? You can't walk your ass around here alone in the dark, bro. Look, man, I..."

Levi pushes him back, not taking anything he's saying into consideration. His only concern is getting Séa back alive, and if he can get to that conclusion faster, then he will – even by doing it alone. "No, Coe, man. Stay here with Maria, and y'all case this first floor while I hit the second. We'll holler if we find her, got it?" He looks back at his old friend who for the first time has doubt and death written all across his face, like he knows in his heart of hearts that he will never see his friend again. Levi doesn't allow Roscoe's appearance to change his mind, so he concludes the conversation. "I'm coming back, man. Shit," he smiles although it's forced. "It's me, man. Ain't nobody ever kick my ass. Let's do this." He looks over at Maria. "I'm gonna move faster than you two, so by the time I get back, you guys should still be looking. Holler at me every two minutes, and I'll hit you back. I promise."

Although Roscoe doesn't want to rationalize the idea of splitting up with Levi, he knows it's probably the only best idea that's available. The sooner they find Séa, the better the chances of her being alive, and they can carry both Séa and Maria to the front gates and escape. The fact that Maria is walking full of meds and pain after being shot in the back means that time will be wasted if they have to cope with her as she slugs along. She can't be left alone either, therefore, Roscoe ends up agreeing with Levi although it's obvious that he doesn't like it

He holds out his hand to the man he has seen as his brother for so long, even through the time when they were incommunicado. They hug, and then he watches as Levi disappears into the darkness, only his footsteps being heard until even that sound silences. He looks back at Maria who already is sniffling, therefore, he chooses to look beyond her to stay on the task at hand which is Séa.

"Every two minutes, Maria. Keep count and don't forget. You walk close to the wall, and I'll walk right beside you. Stay up with me, and hold the wall to help you when you feel pain." Roscoe guides her over to the wall, starting at the entrance so that they can move forward. The place is formed in the shape of a circle, and as they walk forward, they consistently pass by doors that are of equal distance apart. As they pass each door, they check if each door is unlocked, but no door opens.

"Levi!"

Absolutely no time passes before they hear Levi yell back. "I'm good!" Then, there's more silence as his echo fades.

"What do we do if he doesn't answer, Roscoe?" she whispers.

Roscoe stops in his tracks, but after about two seconds, he keeps moving, giving her no response.

"Séa?" Levi calls, highly guarded against an attack from who Maria has introduced as the killer of the Doons as he holds his gun in both his hands. Although Levi never wants a career in law enforcement, he knows all the moves of a police officer after being semi-trained by the same uncle who gets him slaps on the wrists whenever he commits a misdemeanor. "Séa!"

Each step feels heavier than the one before it as he attempts to open each door he passes so that he can get a better look inside. There are windows at the top of each door, however, with no real light, it's impossible for him to see any shadow, much less a real live body. Feeling discouraged, the further he moves in his attempt to find Séa, he has to cover his nose as the stench he encountered when he first opened the huge, gold plated doors grows stronger. It's so strong until he begins to cough as he tries to hold his breath long enough to get through it.

"What is that smell?" he asks himself as he squints his eyes while fanning the pistol in front of his face. As he approaches the next door, he wiggles the knob, and it opens, causing him to dismiss, for only a couple of seconds, the nauseating smell that has taken over his nostrils. As he walks inside, he hears another call.

"Levi!" calls Maria from the bottom floor, but when Levi hears her voice, he loses footing and trips up on an elevated portion of the floor, catching himself on the balcony's rail.

"Yeah! Yeah, I'm cool!" he shouts back. He turns his attention back to the open room, aiming his pistol at nothing but hoping for something that acts, thinks and moves like the man who took the life of his cousin so that he can repay the favor.

Careful not to trip up again, he moves into the room easily with the pressure of remaining in control. It's not simple to ignore the stench that is getting stronger and more potent than ever before with every inch of floor he covers, so he decides to hold his breath until forced to breathe again. Using his ears more than his eyes, he calls on Séa again before bumping into a table. Completely blinded, he runs his hand across the table, trying to find the edge of it so that he can go around. While his fingertips carve out every detail of the wood that juts out from the table's edge, they also begin to feel the warmth of blood flowing down a limp wrist.

"Oh God, Séa," he mumbles as his eyes become a dam for tears. Immediately, his pistol goes into the front of his pants, and he maneuvers the body upward while he cries her name. This all comes to halt when, as he grabs her from behind to slide her from the table, his hands rest on her chest and then long, flowing hair falls onto his arms. Just as quickly as he picked the bloody body up, he drops it onto the floor, the head dangling like

128

a medallion from his ankle. It's not Séa. He kicks the body off of him, and that's when he hears a noise from behind. Ripping the gun from his pants, he turns around and fires without any hesitation.

"Levi! Levi!" Maria screams, placing her hands over her ears and cowering in fear at the sound of a gunshot. She falls to the floor and begins to go hysterical all over again, afraid of what has happened as she continues to call Levi, but he won't answer.

Roscoe, who was once full of confidence, for the first time breaks down when he doesn't hear Levi respond to Maria's call. His chest begins to go up and down like a mad man, and his rage is flared up uncontrollably as he calls only once more for his silenced friend. "Levi!" His powerful cry echoes throughout the entire place, but Levi's voice is nowhere to be heard. Without turning back at Maria, he begins to walk back toward the stairs that took Levi to his destination.

"Don't leave me here!" Maria cries, but Roscoe only stops to respond coldly.

"Don't leave you here? If your stupid ass would have stopped mumbling back there and got your ass in the truck..." he pauses while his heart feels like it's about to explode. Then, he quiets down. "No, you find your ass a way out of here by yourself. We're not stopping for your ass anymore."

"Please, Roscoe!"

He ignores her as she grovels behind him, begging him not to leave her alone. As he disappears into the shadows, Maria stands to her feet with nowhere to go, in disbelief at how Roscoe blames her for all that's going on. In desperation, after standing there for a couple of minutes, she grips the arrow and starts to walk carefully in the same direction as Roscoe because she has no way to get over the outside gate alone. That's when a voice calls.

"I will kill you, Maria," someone sings quietly. "Shhhh, don't move," the voice orders, getting louder upon approach.

Maria starts to run but stops in her tracks when the voice meets up with her head on. Her knees buckle, and then she suddenly wets herself. The urine puddles onto the floor, flowing down her thighs and even inside her shoes, but even in her shallow breaths and all the wetness, she lifts her arrow directly in front of herself. As she aims only in the direction of the voice she hears, the voice starts talking again. This time, the voice is in a much higher, tenor pitch, one that's taunting and meant to jeer at her in the worst way.

"I'm going to kill you, Maria."

"Roscoe! Levi!" she cries, but her whimper barely reaches beyond herself due to an absolute fear crippling her speech.

"Can you see me, Maria?" he heckles, but Maria can't see him anywhere, not until he tells her which way to look. "Turn around, Maria."

The tone of his voice changes again, growing husky with more influence of supremacy over her. Instead of turning around, Maria tries to bolt forward, but the man uses only his voice to stop her. She's so terrified that she freezes. Not even the muscles in her throat can force her to utter a sound.

"Now turn around and look at me quietly or I will kill you," he utters slowly, and Maria turns around. Her legs shake so badly that they're knocking against one another. Her bowels have already started to loosen, and now they are leaking all over her legs. As her eyes return a stare back at the same face she saw murdering Pierre, she begins to cry, her throat going into convulsions.

"Duck, duck, duck..." he repeats as he walks around her, placing his finger up underneath her chin, motioning her to follow him. Maria somehow forgets that she has the arrow in her hand aimed straight at him, but as he's softly walking and repeating duck, duck, duck, she remembers. They go around and around, and there's no clue as to when he will stop. He simply walks and repeats the words of a game that children play, and as he continues, Maria gets a firmer grip on the arrow. She stares back at the only things that she can see in the darkness which are the whites of his eyes, and she finally throws her arm forward, aiming for his stomach.

He moves back, looks down at the arrow, and then back up at her face which has fallen into a state of even more distress after missing the man she wants to kill. As he watches her prepare to swing at him again, he replies, "Goose!"

"Nooo!" she screams, but it's too late. He raises a machete and swings at his target. Upon impact, Maria's screaming head falls to the ground as her body drops immediately inside her waste.

Chapter Eight

"Levi? Levi?" Roscoe whispers, walking fast and ignoring the scream from Maria downstairs, believing that it's coming only because he left her alone. In his heart, Levi, Pierre and Séa put their lives on the line for her, and he did also. Therefore, Maria truly has to fend for herself. Although he is trying not to do so, he resents Maria with everything inside of him.

Suddenly, he hears whimpering from a room he passes by and stops cold in his tracks because it sounds like Séa. He turns the knob on the door, but it doesn't open. Before trying to knock it down, he scans the area around him to be sure he has enough time to respond in case the man trying his best to kill them returns. When he sees the coast is clear, he raises his leg and kicks the door three times. On the third time, it flies open, but once he is able to look into the room, it's too dark to make out the vague image on the floor in the corner. Therefore, he walks toward the small whimper with his knife ready to plunge into someone's body in self defense. It's only then does he recognize that the whimper isn't anything nor anyone to defend himself from. It's Séa.

Immediately he turns around to check his rear and then gets down onto one knee with her. "Séa, take your hands down from your face, baby. It's me, Roscoe. Baby, look at me."

He places his hands on top of hers and removes them from her face so that she can understand that she's not alone and that she'll be okay. As her hands come down, she looks back into his eyes and starts to cry louder, so he puts his hand over her mouth. That doesn't work well, so he leans over and whispers in her ear something that she's wanted to hear for a long time. It's a secret that she and Roscoe have kept from everyone and even tucked it in the back of their own thoughts, playing things off to keep everyone at peace. To them, they are taking one for the team, but inside, their hearts race for one another, despite how much they care for Levi.

"Séa, baby, please, you have to be quiet. I love you. I do, but we have to find Levi and get out of here. That's my boy, and I know we were gonna allow ourselves this vacation to sort out our feelings, but right now, I need you to come back to me. Pretend like it's just you and me now so we can go, alright? Quiet down. Can you do that for me? As soon as you see Levi, he's back on take over." Then, he kisses her on her lips, and she kisses him back. She then backs away to gather herself together the best she can.

"Where *is* Levi, Coe?"

"Man, I don't know. I'm looking for him, too."

"I heard his gun. Roscoe, he can't be dead because he fired his gun," she panics.

"I know, Séa, so get up. The problem is that he isn't answering. We gotta find him." He stops, turns toward the door and then back at Séa. "How did you get away?"

She stares back at him plainly and said, "I ran. When he turned, I just broke free and ran. Coe, he was gonna kill me," she sobs. "He was gonna just kill me for nothing," she states, shaking and scared. "He's crazy…"

"Shh!" He pushes Séa back down into the corner.

"Roscoe! Roscoe!"

As soon as Roscoe hears the call, he storms out of the room. It's Levi, and he sounds very close, like he's in the next room. In fact, when Roscoe leaves from Séa's side, as soon as he exits and turns the corner, he looks to the left and spots a figure in the middle of the floor, stumbling a little but holding on to the railing that blocks anyone from falling to the first floor.

"Levi," Roscoe calls, walking over to the figure cautiously, but when he is certain that it's Levi, he drags him into the room with himself and Séa, shutting the door behind him. Unfortunately, the door has no lock anymore since he kicked it in, so he has no choice but to shove the knife under it while he gets Levi situated.

"Where's your gun?" Roscoe asks as he stands Levi up.

"Ahhh!" Levi moans, grabbing his leg. "I shot at something. Something moved, and then it moved across my damn foot, man, and I shot my damn self!" He props himself up on the wall. "I don't know what the hell to do, man, but this thing hurts like hell. There's even a dead ass body back there, bleeding and all. We gotta get out of here," he continues until he hears Séa's voice.

"Levi?" She gets up, rushing over to him with a warm embrace and kiss on the cheek. "I heard your gun go off and..."

"Yeah, and what you just heard is what happened. I got shook and shot my damn self. You alright, baby? He didn't hurt you?"

"No, no. I got away." She looks up at Roscoe whom she knows is concentrating on being the look-out, trying not to ever look her way too much. With the history of the two men standing before her, now would not be the time for this type of war. The true war is getting out of the Doons alive. "I'm just glad you're alive, baby." She reaches around his neck, and he reciprocates with a hug around the waist.

Roscoe interjects, "We gotta go."

"Where's Maria?"

"Yeah, where is she?" inquires Séa right after Levi's question. Roscoe stands tall to answer.

"I figured when the gun went off and you didn't answer that I could find you much quicker alone than with her. I thought it was either you or the killer that got shot, and when you didn't answer..." He glances Séa's way, but quickly adjusts back to Levi, pretending to crack his neck. Levi knows him all too well, and since this is the first time they've been together in a while, the last thing he wants to do is allow Levi to catch him in even a small daze over Séa.

"Maria!" Séa immediately calls, but Levi silences her.

"Let's just go back down. We can get her real quick." Levi stands taller in efforts to show he is still strong enough for the task, tolerating the pain that comes with a shot to the leg. "Séa, she's by herself. Don't call her. We don't know where that fool ass killer is. If she hollers back, he'll know for sure and will probably kill her, too, if he hasn't already."

"Why'd you leave her, Roscoe?" she cries. Then she reaches back and slaps the heck out of his face. "Why the hell did you leave Maria back there to fuckin' die, Roscoe! She's wounded dammit!"

"Whoa, Séa! Back up," Levi states, grabbing her arm so that she won't hit him again. "The point was to come and find you, and we had a plan," he glances at Roscoe who nods back at him. "They had to split. If Roscoe made that decision, then I have to believe that it was the best one. Babe..." He turns her face toward his, breaking the stare between herself and his friend. "There are only so many options, and this is the last one we have – to get to Maria before she gets killed. She's probably hiding out. She can't be just out in the open. She's not stupid, Séa," he explains again. "Roscoe had to come find us because he had no choice." This Levi says only to calm Séa, but he has his secret reservations about Roscoe's reasoning.

Before heading on their way out, Levi notices how Roscoe's eyes follow Séa. She walks around to hold on tightly to the arm of her main boyfriend Levi, but her eyes are positioned toward the floor. Levi notices that as well, but he says nothing. When Roscoe looks away, ready to lead the way out, his eyes make a staggering halt onto Levi's eyes, so he immediately says something foul to divert the attention away from Levi's unique gift of discernment.

"Tell that girl she better keep her hands to her damn self." Then he walks off, knife in the air, trying to keep himself alive, but unfortunately, there's a nagging thought inside of his head about what Levi is thinking as he follows him closely behind with the woman he happens to be in love with on his arm.

It was last year when Levi'd gotten locked up on some misdemeanor crime over the weekend when Roscoe noticed how sad Séa had been getting over many things. First it was the death of Justynn, and then, according to the information that he knew through Pierre, Levi just wasn't there for her. He tapped out emotionally. At that same time, Roscoe and his girl at the time, Janet, were going through drama, and in the midst of all of the confusion, Roscoe went weak for Séa. Séa also went weak for Roscoe, and it all started right outside of the jailhouse as they stood in support of the one friend they both loved most – Levi. No, Levi and Roscoe weren't talking at all at the time, but Roscoe still tried his best to get back on the right ground with Levi, or so it seemed. Actions and emotions between Roscoe and Séa fell into territories that were strictly forbidden, therefore, they

138

planned to never tell. Now, it's gone too long and hard, and a decision must be made.

"Step," Roscoe whispers as he and Séa both guide Levi down the staircase so he won't fall with his shot leg. The last thing they need is to have to carry Levi all the way to the road, especially with Séa's leg badly bruised by the heel of a shoe. As Roscoe checks both sides of the staircase, he calls Maria, but gets no answer, figuring that she left like he advised her to do before letting his anger guide him away from her. He regrets the situation now more than ever.

"Maria, girl, it's me, Séa," she calls in a low tone trying not to dignify her cry with tears, but she feels deep down in her gut that her long time friend has joined Justynn in heaven. "Maria," she calls as she takes another step down, closing in on the floor when she steps on top of something that feels like a ball, nearly causing her to fall. Levi leans over to grab her, almost falling himself when Séa begins to scream bloody murder. "Maria!" she cries over and over again as she stands atop of the loose strands of her friend's hair which are attached to the detached head on the floor of the Doons.

Vomit spills onto the floor after Séa trips up again, this time onto her decapitated body. Falling to the floor, Séa screams while Roscoe and Levi stand stunned at the mangled body of Maria in front of them, but all the attention is turned away from her in a split second. There's a sickened heckle coming from the shadows directly behind Séa.

Roscoe and Levi both leap to grab Séa, and although their lives are hanging by the balance due to a killer standing before them, Levi notices when Séa reaches forward, her arms attach to Roscoe's, not his. He pauses only for one second over the incident, but then raises his pistol and fires directly in the direction of the heckle as Séa hustles to her feet.

"Go! Go!" Levi shouts and watches her let go of Roscoe's hands to head for the entrance to escape. When she gets there with the door wide open, she yells back at them both.

"Come on! Levi, Roscoe...come on!" she screams at the top of her lungs as the veins pop through her neck. Her body tenses up, knowing that she can't make it without them. She watches as both of them back up toward the door, ready to fight or kill if need be. In the midst of saving her own life and trying to save theirs as well, she realizes that they both love her, and she also loves both of them. Then, she cuts her eyes back at Maria's body on the floor, and an ultimate fear rises back up inside her body that makes her call for the two loves of her life again. "Please! Just run!"

"Get the fuck outta here, man," orders Levi to Roscoe, and Roscoe turns to him in disbelief.

"What? Bring your ass outta here with me, or..."

"What the fuck you think? I'm not coming?" Levi shouts back, looking straight forward into the darkness for the hidden voice. "No," he breathes heavily, "I'm coming," he says with certainty. "I'm just the one with the pistol though." He cuts his eyes at him quickly, ignoring his suspicious thoughts for now, and then stares back ahead. "You be my back up and stay with Séa. Get her across that gate first then hook me up."

Roscoe immediately does what Levi suggests because it all makes sense or else they would be trapped inside the gates. As Roscoe runs to meet Séa, Levi glances back in a split second to see Roscoe grab her hand to head out the door. When he turns back around, the image of the man who murdered Maria and Pierre enters into the view given by the moonlight., however, right before Levi gets the opportunity to pull the trigger, the man moves into the darkness becoming invisible. At that, Levi moves backwards quickly, goes through the entrance, and Roscoe is there at the gate waiting to lift him over.

Levi hobbles down the steps with the gun pointing up into the sky as Roscoe prepares to give him a boost. He glances down at Roscoe while stepping on his back. Then he leans and jumps over the gate, falling down to his knees when he hits the ground due to his shot leg. He quickly gets up after taking a look at Séa standing near a tree, and then points the gun.

Roscoe grabs the top of the gate where there are tips missing, but before he climbs, his eyes meet the barrel of Levi's gun.

"Shit," he falls backwards to the ground, but quickly gets back up to watch Levi turn the pistol away from him and at the large doors that they just exited. Although he believes he really saw Levi aiming the gun at him, he forgets about it and hops the gate, pissed but keeping focus on getting out of the Doons alive.

"Let's get the hell out of this place." Levi doesn't hesitate to start jogging on his hurt leg through the trees when Roscoe stops him.

"Through the trees?"

"Where the hell else? Do you want him to shoot a damn arrow in your back like he did Maria? With trees separating us from him, at least we have a shot at losing him, or we have something to block us. Now let's go." He looks over. "Come on, Séa."

She doesn't hesitate to join Levi as they run into the wooded area in hopes to be headed toward the main entrance at the road. There's enough room in between the trees for a clear run, but so dark that it's easy to lose direction. When Séa looks back, she notices that Roscoe follows closely behind. Even though they are making good distance in between themselves and the killer, Levi suddenly stops his run.

"Baby, you okay? We gotta keep going," Séa asks, panting and ready to go further. "We can do it," she continues, reaching up to his face, concerned that he may be giving up or in too much pain to continue on his leg. "You're the strongest man I know."

"Am I?" His eyes cut deeply into her soul, and she removes her hands from his face while he turns to face the man he thought was his friend once again. Roscoe stops in his tracks, looks back behind himself, and then back at Levi whom he now knows is pointing the pistol directly at him. "Do you fuckin' think I'm crazy as hell, man? It looks like the pressure of this fucked up vacation got to you, huh?"

142

"Levi, stop it!" Séa shouts angrily.

"Séa, you fuck him?"

"What?" she asks, backing up and taken by complete surprise by his question. Then, she looks back at Roscoe whose shoulders aren't as broad anymore but appearing more crushed as he consumes the words that have come from Levi's mouth to her.

"Why the long ass pause?" A tear falls from his left eye as he looks at them both. He then wipes his face, ashamed of the tears he is giving to Roscoe. "How long y'all been fuckin'?"

"Levi, it's time to go man. We have to keep going. Pierre's down, and..."

He walks closer to Roscoe, and Séa dares not touch him to cause interference. Instead, she backs into a tree, still reaching out helplessly to Levi, but her mouth refuses to make a sound. She can't believe that Levi figured it out, and she begins to rethink all the moves she's made on the trip or if she's even said anything to throw him any hints. It's at this moment that she's very much aware of the danger Roscoe is in. Along with being a hot head and outside of clowning around, whatever Levi says, he means. Wherever he points that pistol, he'll shoot.

Séa grips the tree's bark, and it begins to crumble inside the palms of her hands. A sickening sensation grows in the pit of her stomach, and she sinks to the ground trying to gather the strength to run in front of the barrel of the gun. Her feet just won't let her, much less the fear that quakes inside her soul when she imagines life without either one of them as a result of her lies and indiscretions.

"Please, please, Levi," she speaks, suffocating on her own breath as the seconds go by, each one potentially fatal.

"You would never do that to me, man? Ain't that what the fuck you said back there? Is that why you couldn't wait to make me look like the bad guy in front of Séa earlier when I got into the squabble with my own flesh and blood? What..." he says, glancing at his girlfriend as she crotches at the tree. "You're in love with her, too?"

"Levi, put the gun down, man. We got a killer out here...we can sort this out..."

"The hell you think?" Levi can hold back his tears no longer. They come streaming down his face, completely taken by the death around him and the fact that he knows beyond a doubt that the woman he loves is sleeping with his best friend. "My cousin's dead over there in a fuckin' rental ass truck, and hell, the trick you were supposed to be hooking up with got her damn head rolling on the fuckin' floor, and to top this off...I saw the way you and Séa looked at each other." He turns tearfully to the side to talk to Séa. "What happened to me, huh? You grabbed his arms to have him pull you up when it's me that's was willing to die for your ass up in there? What? Your ass think I'm stupid, or you got this idea that he's better...that he really fuckin' loves you?" Then he yells louder than he's ever yelled before. "You don't know shit about that man, Séa! I was right about his ass.

He's not the same man." He cuts his eyes at Roscoe. "Because he's too busy trying to be the man I am."

"Levi, please, don't…"

"No, I'll tell you what *don't*… This brother right here better *don't* move one more time toward me or this man you love so much gonna get blasted."

"Levi, come on!" Roscoe yells at the top of his lungs. "Man, let's go. We don't have time for this shit!" His fists ball up and his chest begins to swell. "We got a mother fucker out here that already killed two of us, and now you're pointing a gun at me? At me, man?" he repeats in disbelief. Then, he walks forward, unafraid of the pistol that stares him in the face and even greater, unafraid to take the bullet to possibly die. "Give me this damn gun….got time for this shit."

Levi just stands there, holding the pistol directly at his chest as he approaches, and on the sidelines, Séa screams for Levi not to shoot him. The more she screams for Roscoe's life, the more enraged Levi becomes, realizing even through his anger that she really cares for him that much. Roscoe takes one more step closer and reaches for the gun, but that's when Levi drops his arm, only as a result of Séa's pleas which prove he'll do anything for her. The pistol aims at the ground.

"Didn't I tell you not to point that mother fuckin' gun at me again, man? I should beat your ass right now, but I'll save that shit until we leave. Yeah," he looks at Séa who is sobbing heavily but still trying to check for the killer who could be somewhere close to them in the dark. "I love Séa, and I made love to her, too, a multitude of times. How's that? Now point that pistol at me again and watch me smoke your ass with it."

Levi weakly stares over at Séa, ignoring the threat he considers empty coming from Roscoe who stands an inch out of arms length away from him. He could care less about Roscoe or his words because he knows it's all for show. His heart has been destroyed by the only woman he's ever loved. As Séa stares back at Levi, she understands the question that he's asking without his use of words, and she nods her head. He, then, wipes his face, turns back to Roscoe, and walks off with his eyes glued to Séa.

"If you love him..." Levi states quietly.

"Levi," Séa calls, going after him, but he raises his pistol.

"Back up, Séa. Y'all asses grinning in my face...and that's why your ass didn't want me to put him down on the balcony over there. Now, I said back the hell up Séa. You don't want what I got for your ass." He looks back at Roscoe one last time. "I can find my own way out."

He leaves them behind, never looking back while the woman he loves stands next to the man she chose over him, if only for a moment in time. Roscoe doesn't give Séa one glance. Instead, he locks his fingers into hers, being careful to not deplete himself of his senses behind Levi's stunt. He knows that there's a real killer on the loose, and he has to get Séa and himself out of there. As he starts running, Séa has no choice but to follow him as they run in another direction toward the entrance with her heart burdened in sorrow while toiling over her decision to be with Roscoe when she still has strong feelings for Levi.

As she runs with Roscoe through the trees, she watches his motions as he moves through the trees like an eagle. No matter how dark it is, it's like he can see just like it's daylight out. He's running so fast that she can barely keep up, and when she stumbles, he jerks her arm, forcing her to catch her balance and continue to move.

"Roscoe, Roscoe, wait. I'm tired and my leg is too sore," she complains out of breath. "We have to be going the wrong way because it's taking too long. Let's go the way Levi went..."

"What?" he stops and turns to face her, irritated with the way things are going. "Didn't you see him? This man pointed a gun at you, too, Séa. Looks to me like we have two people out here in this damn wilderness that want us to take our last breaths, and you're talking about following him?"

"He wasn't gonna shoot me..."

"Yet.," he interrupts. "You don't know him like I do. He needs to cool off. He's hot headed."

She removes her hand from his. "And what about you, Roscoe? Don't be so quick to judge him." Then she looks behind herself into the night, wondering about Levi's well being.

"Judge him? Are you serious?"

"Look, Roscoe, he's hurt! We should just go back to find him is all I'm saying!"

"Did that man look like he was poking along to you, huh? I know Levi. That wound isn't gonna stop him. He'll shake that off and keep moving. Did you not see him? He's probably at the damn gate before us!" Roscoe then looks around. "It does look like we are going in the wrong direction though. Let's turn up this way."

Before they start to move again, they hear a crack in the fallen leaves. Immediately, they turn around, looking every which way. Still, they see nothing.

"Shit, Roscoe, shit!" Séa panics, grabbing his arm because she simply doesn't know what else to do.

"Shhh! Be quiet," Roscoe delivers. "Stand back." He pushes her behind him and tells her to look around. If anything moves, she's to let him know fast. Roscoe's knife is already in his hand and ready to do some damage.

Before Roscoe stops speaking, Séa already has the drop on what's going on around her. Unable to scan quickly because of the unfamiliar surroundings, she's careful to only look for one thing – the killer. She could care less about any stray animals or the constant flurry of leaves that continue to hit her face. The only thing she doesn't want to see close to her or Roscoe is the person Maria called the killer of the Doons.

"I don't see anything, Coe," she verifies.

"Let's walk. This way," he continues, pointing his knife forty degrees another direction. "Keep your ears open. Let me know when you're ready to run again."

It's not even ten steps before they have to slow their gait down to a halt when they hear chopping disturbingly close behind them.

"Simon Says chop," laughs the voice but Roscoe and Séa don't respond to the message out of confusion and fear. Instead, they stare back into the darkness. Each tree coming into their line of vision reveals nothing but itself, and they are so close to one another that Séa's fingers feel the vibration of his heart beating rapidly as she holds on to his mid-back. She steps on a medium sized limb hidden beneath the mud on the drenched ground while she moves into a safer position, and then quickly picks it up. Instead of standing behind Roscoe any longer, she moves back to his side with the full knowledge that she has a better chance of living if nothing happens to him. Therefore, she's ready to defend his life as well as her own with all she has.

The rain starts to pour down again instantaneously as the thunder roars in the sky and the wind picks up speed, churning out a howl that makes an overbearing noise with the rapid crackling of the blowing leaves. There's movement everywhere, but their concentration isn't broken as they stare, searching for the first sign of movement from the threat between the trees. Then, as the noise of nature goes quiet for just one second, coming from directly behind them is a voice so deeply demonic that it sends a chill down Séa's spine.

"Timber." An axe is raised high over the top of Roscoe's head, and before he turns around completely, Séa spins and throws the limb into the killer's face who is only standing three feet behind them. It hits, but the huge man that towers over them doesn't flinch, only stalls, before letting the axe come down. Both Roscoe and Séa fall to the ground as the axe swings, scraping the back of Roscoe, cutting his shirt and slicing his skin wide open. Roscoe yells but continues to move through the rain and mud, his knife sticking out from his hand, as Séa jumps up and begins to pull him the hardest she can as the man raises the axe once again.

"No, God no! Please!" While looking back down at Roscoe she yells, "Move! Get up, Roscoe, get up!"

Roscoe finally finds the strength to maneuver onto his knees, look up at a frantic Séa who is trying to save his life, and then, as he pulls himself up with the help of her strength, he snatches her from her stance only to throw her directly into the axe's path. Séa lands chest first in the mud while Roscoe stands tall, disregarding the wound on his back that's being washed with rain. Séa then sits up onto her knees begging for mercy from the towering demon. Her new love doesn't help her at all. Instead he runs in the other direction. Séa glances back and can hear his footsteps as he disappears, leaving her to die. When she turns back around, she gives up, her head fallen to the ground.

"Please, please," she begs with no other alternative, her voice quivering while the rain pounds onto the back of her body, each time sending jolts of overpowering fear through her body knowing that the next thump could be the axe splitting her apart. Her fingers scrape the tips his boots, and if she stands up, she'll meet her doom face to face. She can't bring herself to move due to the paralyzing terror that overpowers her. "Please, don't kill me. I didn't do anything. I just want to go home," she sobs, praying to God that He might set her free, and she starts to pray aloud. "Please, forgive me, Jesus. Forgive me, and please help me..."

From out of nowhere, a gunshot rings out, and Séa's body bawls up in a knot as the magnitude of her scream carries throughout the trees. Her body quakes on the ground as her hands cover her ears to block out the doom that she feels about to come. Another gunshot goes off and finally, she feels the movement of the killer's feet back away.

"Séa, back up! Back up!"

"Levi! Levi, oh God, Levi!" she screams, mud and rain covering her body. She doesn't even look up to see where the killer went before she backs up. Her knees dig into the mud until Levi walks closer to pull her up with one arm. Her body collapses onto him in full sorrow as he holds onto her tightly, in total opposition to the pain in his leg that wants to relax and fall over to the ground.

"Let's go."

"I'm so sorry, Levi. I'm sorry, please forgive me," Séa cries. "I didn't mean to hurt you..."

"Enough of that. I gotta get you out of here," he breathes heavily. He grabs Séa's face and wipes it down with his bare hands. "Are you hurt?"

"No," she responds, "Not anything more than my leg, but I can run."

"Well, I need that woman that I know you can be and that you are. Lead us out of here. I got the back. I don't know how much longer I can go on this leg, baby, because my adrenaline is leaving. I can feel it. The way out is that way." He points forward. "Now let's go. I don't know if I shot him because he's not down. He's somewhere, but he's not down."

Before starting on her way, Séa's sorrowful look into Levi's eyes speaks volumes, so he answers.

"I always promised you I would take care of you. I ain't the best man, but I'm a man of my word to the lady I love. I saw Roscoe on the way here. He stopped in his tracks cold and shrugged like he lost you. When I didn't see you with him..." His lip starts to quiver. "I still love you, Séa. I thought he lost you or that you were dead, and I couldn't..."

"No, Levi. He didn't lose me. He left me back here alive," Séa corrects him with tears streaming down her face along with the rain. Her heart is bursts from the betrayal that has her on both ends – one from Roscoe and the other she gave to Levi. "He left me alive so that I could die! He set me up, threw me on in front of him when he'd gotten chopped with the axe."

152

"That mother ..." he starts, becoming more enraged than a caged beast, but he regroups, finally satisfied that Séa sees who Roscoe really has become over the years. Then, they both continue to run in the direction that Levi believes will take them to the path that leads to the front gates. He feels down in his pocket for an extra clip because in the back of his mind, he hopes to see Roscoe once more, even more than his hopes to see the killer, so he can unload his last round on him for throwing Séa to her death.

Chapter Nine

Out of breath, Roscoe continues to run, satisfied with how he left Séa back there to die. After thinking about how he misled Levi once again by not even saying a word and making him believe that he lost Séa in the woods is yet another win for him. How Levi actually fell for it, he believes that he has Levi in the palm of his hand on any matter because Levi has always been too emotional.

"His stupid ass. Who's the better man now…smarter, too? It's time for me to get the hell up outta here," he says quietly to himself as he feels around, realizing that he's started back over from the beginning. "This is the way we should have gone in the first place, right back up this path," he continues as he jumps back on the trail that leads to the abandoned houses.

As he searches the immediate area, he doesn't see a threat so he uses his knife to cut his shirt off and tie it around his stomach. The pain is increasing at his back where he was cut, and he can feel the blood running down his pants. Despite it all, his confidence is at one hundred percent, and he can taste his way out of the Doons.

Approaching the house, he spots all the photography equipment they left behind while they were trying to get away the first time. Instead of going inside the house, he chooses to take the route he already has traveled which is around the side of the house, the same way Maria led them. His soaked pants weigh down heavy on him, and now he can't tell the difference between his blood and the rain because they're both the same temperature.

"Lemme get my stuff," he says under his breath as he approaches the abandoned SUV that still contains his dead friend Pierre. As he walks beside the leaning vehicle, he doesn't even look inside. Instead, he looks away, sliding his hand into the ajar driver's side window to shake it until it comes off line. When the window falls inside the door's panel, he pops the trunk to retrieve a wind breaker and some socks. From there, he pads his back with the socks to stop the bleeding, ties the shirt back around his stomach, puts on the jacket and sets off on a clear path toward the barren highway as fast as he can.

"There it is. You see it?"

"No, Levi, I don't," strains Séa who refuses to allow herself to slow Levi up. As he struggles to run, Séa performs like a trooper, having him lean on her for more endurance. The only problem is that she doesn't know how much longer she can help him out at this fast rate without a break.

"I see a brick wall over there, and if we follow it, there should be the opening where we drove in here."

"Okay, but I don't know how much longer I can stand tall like this without a break."

Levi looks back and doesn't see a threat in sight, so they stop and take a break. "We can take a break right here. Just keep your eyes open for the crazy mo' fucker, and I'll keep my eyes open for somebody else."

Séa glances down at the gun that's firmly gripped in his left hand, and she's aware that if Levi sees either one, he's killing them both...or at least he's going to try. Although she still had feelings for Roscoe over ten minutes ago, those feelings are all gone as a result of him tossing her over to death just to save his own life. Levi was right. He's always been right about his instincts. Roscoe has changed for the worse.

"Are you ready?" he asks as the rain comes to a slow down.

"Yeah, I can go further now."

"When we get to the brick wall, walk that shit fast. Don't worry about me. I'll be there, right behind you, pistol out and ready to kill a mo' fucker that tries some shit."

"Why do you want me to run ahead of you? What kind of sense does that make?"

"Just do as I say. You're a female. I'm the bait. He wants me first so he can easily get to you. If some ill shit happens, you'll at least have distance between us.

Maria said this damn lunatic was a stalker and he knew shit about the people he killed. All that means is that he's watching us if I didn't wound him bad back there." Levi stops talking and glances up at the nighttime sky, obviously making a short and silent prayer to God. "I need to go back to church."

"I know that's where I'm going when I get outta here. Every Sunday! The front row."

"Yeah, Bible open!"

They laugh only for a brief moment and give each other the much needed small kiss before starting on their way.

"I got confused, Levi," Séa confesses, "I let my guard down and..."

"And Roscoe did what he does best. Same crap he did with the last girl I was with. He may be suave, but I'm down like four flats are supposed to be for you, babe. I forgive you though, and I never stopped loving you...even back there."

"I know you didn't, and I regretted doing everything I'd done the moment I thought I'd lost you. I love you, Levi, and I was just too stupid to realize how much."

"You're just saying that because I saved your life back there," he kids.

"No, I'm not!"

"Just playing with you," he pauses and kisses her again. "I saw it in your eyes. I know you still loved me. You never could hide it." He turns to look back again. "Let's go before we get chopped up out here like some dumb asses that stop to make love while a killer is on their trail."

"Stop! You hear that?" she says leaning up against the brick wall.

"Yeah, it sounded like a car. Come on let's go. We're too close to the road to slow it up now."

As Roscoe runs at a steady, rhythmic pace down the dirt road, not giving way to his wet trunks and shoes, he starts to hear the sound of more footsteps somewhere behind him. Immediately, he stops and reverses direction, and when he does, the foreign footsteps halt as well. His eyes are peeled, and even though there's only a light sprinkle, it makes seeing beyond the mist in the darkness no easier.

When he sees nothing, he turns back around and keeps going, attributing it to possible paranoia, but then he hears it again. With each step he takes, another step comes, but off of his rhythm. Roscoe knows it's him. He's been watching him the whole time, and this is just another one of his games before he kills.

"Keep running, Roscoe," he says, convincing himself that he has the upper hand. The chase begins to take another form the closer Roscoe gets to the road which he can see as clear as day whenever a stray car drives by. The footsteps behind him gain speed resulting in Roscoe picking up speed as well, but he can't run as fast as the steps coming after him. Therefore, he stops, out of breath, but ready to fight. When he turns around, who he thought was behind him is actually beside him. The killer moves out from beyond the trees before Roscoe's very eyes.

Roscoe lifts his knife, and his adrenaline pushes him to attack before being attacked. Before Roscoe leaps forward in defense, he stalls to watch the hooded, blood thirsty psychopath lift his hand and press a button resulting in a noise that comes from over his shoulder. When Roscoe peers to his right through his periphery, the gates that were once open to the road start to close.

"Shit!" Immediately, he takes off in a mad dash for the road as his exit becomes more and more a dead end. Behind him, he feels the rapid approach of the man who is succeeding at playing with his mind. The closer Roscoe gets to the gate, the more his hopes of getting out dwindle as he measures the gate's height visually. He figures that he will need help getting over if he doesn't make it through before they seal shut. When he sees the top of the gate clearly in the night as he gets within ten feet of it, he angers on the inside, boiling over as it seals shut before him. That's when he tightens the grip on his knife, turns around and swings at the man who has chased him all the way up the path. He misses the face of his assailant but comes back with an uppercut as the killer comes back with an axe to Roscoe's stomach creating a wound so big that blood and organs begin to leak out. He grabs at his stomach, the inside and outside, when he breathlessly watches the killer pull the axe back again ready to strike. That's when he hears a scream – Séa's scream. Roscoe weakly glances to the left and sees the woman he left for the kill, and now it's her who watches as the killer slices Roscoe's whole body in half. The upper half of Roscoe's body falls to the ground, his eyes set on Séa, and his legs still standing.

"Run!" Séa screams to Levi as he stares on in agony at the sight of the man he wanted to hate and love like a brother all at the same time just die at the hands of the sociopath that is now marching toward them. "Stop staring, Levi, and run!" Séa shouts again, yanking his arm, but to no avail.

"Come on, psycho-fuckin-path," he waves the killer his way as he points his pistol directly at his chest. "I can shoot this fool right now, Séa! Let me go!"

Séa falls to the ground as Levi jerks his arm away from her grasp so that he can hit his target easily, just like he was informally trained. He pops off the shot, but the perpetrator continues to come at him like a mad man. Levi, then lets off a couple more shots.

"He's not falling, Séa! Get the hell up and get outta here. He's too close!"

"Come on, Levi!" She rushes to her feet and picks up anything to throw it at the demon that continues to walk through bullets to kill them. "I'm not leaving without you," she screams, "So bring your ass now!"

"Fuck!" He grabs her hand and they run faster than they have before as the killer comes behind them, axe in hand like he's running a marathon. Levi falls over a branch that's in the pathway, dragging Séa down with him, and when she looks back, Levi is already back up on his feet dragging her forward. "Forget that looking back shit. I shot him in the chest. I know I did! He's got to have on a damn vest or some shit to stop those bullets." Levi hears the footsteps coming too close for comfort so without warning Séa, he shoves her behind a tree and locks in on his target's head. He locks eyes with the man he's ready to kill and pulls the trigger, aiming directly at his forehead. The bullet hits, and the man falls backwards to the ground.

Being close to the brick wall, Levi falls against it, finally letting out a breath, shaking and wiping his face with his forearm. This is the first time he's ever killed someone, but he doesn't drop his gun. Instead, he grabs Séa, and they take off toward the front entrance.

"Are you sure he's dead?"

"Hell, yeah. But who the hell cares? We're almost out of this place...Doons, Boons...whatever. Let's just go." He silences as he approaches half of Roscoe's body lying next to the other half of it. He feels Séa squeeze his arm tighter as they hustle to what they find out is a gate that is sealed completely shut.

"What?" Séa asks confused as she shakes the closed gate, but it doesn't move. She begins to kick the wrought iron bars and even reach around on the outside of it for a lock, but she finds nothing. "Levi, do something," she cries, at a total loss for what to do next. As Levi shakes the gate as hard as he can, she looks back where they left their attacker dead and on the ground. He's still there.

"The gate is locked. This gate is seriously locked," Levi exclaims as he follows the height all the way up. "This ain't about nothing!" he complains as he looks around for anything on the side of the gate that would trigger it opening, like a key pad or anything but doesn't find it.

"What do we do, Levi? How do we get out of here, huh?" She continues to look back at the perpetrator, checking to be certain he hasn't moved. Levi notices her.

"He's dead."

"Go shoot him again," she request, but Levi doesn't pay her any attention. She stares him straight in the face and speaks again when he doesn't respond. "Then, give me the gun and let me go blow his damn neck off."

"He's dead, Séa. If he was gonna get up, he would have already. He didn't even toss and turn on the ground when that bullet nailed him. Instead of worrying about a dead man, let's figure out how to get out of here, alright?"

"I just think we should make sure. That's how it is in scary movies," she explains. Although it sounds silly, Séa is serious. "We have to make sure he's dead, babe."

"Séa," he interjects, "This isn't a movie. Calm down," he continues, watching her become consumed with the man who tried to chop her to pieces. "This is real life and bullets kill. Now, let's go." He starts to walk back toward the houses.

"And go where? You know another way out of this place? We're surrounded by a brick wall and iron gates."

"No, but we can find something to help us over the gate. We can't climb these trees and jump, now can we? Let's go."

"Levi, we're right here!" She yells, frustrated that she has to walk away from the closest they've been to freedom.

"And it's not doing us any good, Séa!" he stresses. "What do you think we can do? Squeeze out. There are no cars coming right now, and who says they will stop right here to pick up two people stuck behind a gate in the middle of the freaking Doons if this place is as legendary for murders and shit like Maria said?" He waits on Séa to actually listen to what he's saying, and once he notices that she is softening up, he holds out his hand to her. "Now let's go. It's over. Let's head back to the van."

As he takes her into his arms, he shields her from the two portions of Roscoe that are forever separated, and they walk to the SUV where Levi hopes lies their way out.

"Sit up here and shut the door. I need to get something from the back," he says, only giving a short glance at his dead cousin who lies in the back seat, "So I can cover him up." Séa senses how strong Levi is trying to be, so instead of sitting in the driver's seat, she opens the door back up and decides to help him get whatever he needs to cover Pierre.

After going to the back of the SUV, they grab a crocheted blanket that was packed by Maria and use it to conceal Pierre from their eyesight. Levi fights back the tears while Séa allows them to fall. Then she looks at Levi with full sympathy and lets him know that it's okay. That's when he places his forehead on top of Pierre and weeps bitterly.

"I got him, Peanuts. I got him, man. You sleep good, and I'll see you when I get there, young cousin." He chokes on every word that exits his mouth, and Séa comforts him by caressing his hand.

"Come on. He's coming with us."

"Yeah," Levi responds, wiping his eyes and sniffling to try and gather himself together again. "You know I never really meant any of the things I said to him to break him down. I always played like that with him because I..."

"You loved him. I know. You do the same thing with everyone you love," she comments, referring to herself indirectly. "Come on." Séa climbs into the passenger's seat while Levi gets into the driver's seat despite his leg, and starts up the rental's engine. Séa doesn't argue about who should drive because she senses that he's trying to maintain his sense of manhood that has too often almost been taken away from him during this whole fiasco of a trip.

"Do you think we're gonna make it with the SUV?"

"If we can, as big as the Expedition is, we can bang the gate open, even on these rims, but I really don't even think that will work. If not though, we can climb out on the roof or hood and jump across."

"But your leg…"

"It's a leg, baby. Not the artery in my leg. It'll be alright. I could give a damn if I break it when I jump," he starts to back up slowly, trying not to spin the busted tires and rims in the mud. "I'll hop my ass away from this devil's ground. We'll send help back for Pierre if we have to do the latter."

As Levi turns the steering wheel, the Expedition makes its way to the cleared road. The headlights beam onto the road that reminds them only of escape, a vast difference than what it reminded them of when they decided to turn into the place. At that time, it was similar to a road of refuge.

The rental rides slowly on all three rims and one tire while it feels like the trees that surround them are closing in. Séa continuously checks to be sure the windows are locked as well as the doors. Each time she hits the automatic locks, the clicking sound bothers Levi to the point where he reaches over to hold and rub the back of her hand. Séa maintains her visual, however, making certain that nothing else of any kind comes up to the SUV while they are on their way to the front of the Doons.

Finally, she allows her visual to slip, only a little, when they hit a lower drop in the ground. She glances at Levi who changes the gears, and then she looks back out of the window. Everything is quiet. There is no rain nor are there anymore screams. The silence doesn't put her at ease, and even though Levi holds her hand, she's constantly worried about the truck getting stuck in the ground and most of all, if the man who was running around stalking and attacking them is still lying flat on the ground.

"It's gonna be fine. Sit back."

Séa is leaning forward. The closer they get to the front entrance, the closer she leans to the windshield.

"He's dead, Séa. Let me concentrate on staying on the drier parts of this road," he says, placing the hand that's rubbing her hand back onto the wheel. "I'm paranoid, thinking I feel us sinking, but we're almost there." Levi drives the SUV as close to the trees as he can without running into them. He figures that the soil will be more secure underneath tree roots than out on the dirt road that's filled with sporadic mud spots that luckily, he's missing. The bright lights from the SUV extend enough light that Levi can keep things steady on the ground.

"I don't know, Levi," she pants, her breathing gaining speed as she locates Roscoe's parted body lying in the middle of the street. "We're gonna hit him if we continue to go forward."

"Well that's what we have to do because I'm not going around. I can't do anything about that...just like he couldn't do anything about fixing the shit he did my way. That is if you want to keep it real. The least he can do is be a hard road for us to roll over."

Séa goes silent, knowing that she hasn't a right to tell Levi what to do when it concerns Roscoe, whether he's alive all together in one piece or dead and split up into two pieces. As Levi continues to move the truck forward, she braces herself for what will be Roscoe's chest being crushed by the weight of the SUV. When it hits, she holds her breath and Levi cringes, but before he inches any further up to the gate, Séa looks through her window quickly. As the Expedition drops off of the body, Séa begins to cry out loudly.

"He's not there! We left him there, Levi, and he's not there!" She grabs her chest like she's about to have a heart attack and begins to hit the locks again while checking every area surrounding the truck wildly.

"What do you mean he's not there? You must be looking in the wrong spot," Levi responds, concentrating on getting as close to the gate as he possibly can. "We're gonna get on the roof of this rental and jump over. That way, we can both make it. Roscoe is too close for us to barrel into this gate with enough speed..."

"Levi, I'm serious! He's not there!"

"Bullshit, Séa. Now come on." He unlocks the doors, and Séa immediately locks them back.

"Look!" she screams, and Levi, only now taking her tone seriously, leans over to look out of the window. For about fifteen seconds, he stares at area where he thought the man dropped before they left him there, and even though it's dark, when they were walking away from the scene of the shooting, there was still a big lump on the ground where he lay. After taking in what Séa has been screaming about, Levi slowly sits back in his seat.

"Well?"

Levi retrieves his gun once more, but says nothing to Séa immediately. Instead, he sits back in the seat and shuts his eyes briefly. That's when Séa leans over and smacks him hard on the shoulder.

"Just what the hell are you doing, huh? What the hell are you closing your eyes for when some psycho killer man is out here walking around with a dang bullet in his head like some freaking demon possessed..." she pauses at a loss for descriptive words, but continues, "demon!"

There's a change in Levi, and even though Séa can tell something is going on, she doesn't try to pull it out. She simply waits while on edge, hoping and praying to God nothing else happens while she's waiting. After ten seconds, Levi speaks.

"I need you to get out on the window's ledge, and I'll keep a look out. If you can't jump and pull yourself over the gate when you get to the top of the truck, then I'll boost you up the rest of the way," he says calmly.

"What about you?"

169

"I can get up. I can run hard enough and jump."

"No you can't, Levi! Your leg..."

"Don't tell me what I can't do, baby. I saved you, didn't I? And if I say I'm gonna take care of you, then trust that I will. I'll do it with my life, babe," he continues softly. "Give me kiss right here." He points to his cheek. She then leans over and kisses him. "Now, climb up and over. I'll get out of the truck on your side, and when I see you up and ready, I'll make my way up." Although he tries to make her feel better, she still hesitates.

"I'm scared. I'm really scared, babe." She looks around outside once again. Even though she's right at the gate, it doesn't make her feel better knowing that the killer could be right next to her, unseen and unheard.

"Check this out. Let me get out of the ride, and I'll walk over so I can cover you from the back. We got this," he states calmly, but Séa can't ignore his demeanor.

"What's wrong, Levi, and don't lie to me? Why do you keep looking over there like you can see him?" She points to a portion of the woods that is close to where the killer fell.

"No reason. Just checkin' it out. I'm getting out. Roll your window down. I got you." He kisses her on her lips and then gets out of the SUV, making his way around to her side. When she spots Levi close enough to her door, she slithers her body through the window, and Levi helps her stand on the window's ledge, and she pulls herself up. Then he proceeds to climb up the best way that he can after handing her the gun so that she can watch his back.

"Come on, babe, I got you."

"No, you hold that pistol. Aim that shit behind me, back there where I was looking. You see something move, shoot."

"What?" Séa starts to tremble. "Did you see him? Is he out there?" she asks in full panic mode.

When he gets to the top of the truck, he stands tall and looks at her. "Give me the pistol, Séa. We need to go right now. Kill that panic shit. It won't help." As soon as he grabs the pistol from her, he continues to speak, holding her tightly at her shoulders. "He's out there, Séa. Just don't act like you know he is. Keep looking at me, baby. He's watching. Maria was right about him. He's watching to see who he's gonna try and take next. Don't show your weakness."

Séa glances at his leg quickly and then looks back into Levi's eyes, hopeful that he has a better answer than what she feels he will try to do.

"He already knows about my leg. He saw me leaning on you. He's gonna wait...until I get you over. When you get over, I'm gonna give you the pistol. You shoot if he approaches me, but don't act afraid. This mother fucker senses shit like that I think." Levi stops talking and prompts Séa to climb onto his shoulders. Only half of her body clears the top of the gate, and she dismounts Levi's shoulders to straddle her body through the big gaps that separate the spearheads of the iron gate.

That's when she falls over the top to hit the hard ground hurt, finally free. "Pass me the gun, pass me the gun!" Séa shouts, ignoring the pain of the fall and realizing that time is of the essence. She hasn't even looked up from the ground good yet to see Levi already trying to climb the gate. When she looks over behind him, the killer is charging his way. "Levi!"

"I got this!" he says, "Here! Take the gun!" He tosses Séa the pistol and she allows it to land on the ground. From there, she picks it up and aims at the raging lunatic coming Levi's way.

"I'm gonna shoot!"

"Well, shoot!" he orders, continuing to leap onto the fence, but with nothing to hold on to, he falls.

The gun goes off, but when Levi looks back, the man is still coming, walking like he thirsts for blood. Séa maneuvers closer to the gate, but she's so short that she can't see unless she's backed further away.

"Levi, please, I don't know if I can shoot him!"

Levi jumps one more time, but when he does, he loses his grasp falling on his back directly on the hood of the SUV. He releases a regurgitating moan because the fall directly impacts his shot leg when it slams against the hood. "Pass me the gun, Séa!" he shouts.

She leans in, pressing her full body against the gate to get it back to him, but she can't reach his hand. "Here! Here! This is as far as I can go!"

Levi swings himself around, grabs the pistol, tilts his body up and aims, but when he does, there's nothing to shoot. "Shit! Séa where is he?" He shifts his body to lean his back up against the gate, but when he sees no one still, he pushes himself back up. "Damn!" he shouts, angry at the fact that he hurt his leg worse in the process of it all.

Séa grabs the gate and squeezes tightly, screaming for Levi to just jump. "Hurry! I don't see him! I don't know where he is," she screams, running back and forth in front of the gate trying her best to find him. When she runs to the other side of the gate, she continues to search frantically, helping Levi see from all angles as he stands leaning against the gate. "Levi, just come on, baby," she quiets down as she scoots back directly behind the back of his legs.

As she stands there, she becomes even quieter because for some reason, Levi isn't responding. She tugs on the bottom of his pant legs, still looking, believing that Levi is simply trying to hear versus speak, but that all changes when she hears something fall. When she looks in between Levi's legs, it's the gun. It's fallen out of his hand.

"Levi," she tugs at his leg quietly, and then, she tugs a bit harder, getting sick to the stomach with each passing second that he doesn't respond. "Levi, your gun..."

173

Levi tilts and falls over to the ground, head first from the side of the truck, with a long nail sticking directly out of his forehead. His head lies there leaning on the gate as his body slumps over with no more breath to breathe.

"Levi!" she screams, dropping to her knees and reaching through the wrought iron bars of the gate to adjust Levi's head to see if he's still alive. The tears return as she rocks back and forth, holding her lost love in the palms of her hands while his eyes stare over her shoulder into the dreary sky. Then, a nail hits the iron rail right in front of her, falling directly atop Levi's face.

She falls backwards onto her butt, screaming at the top of her lungs, attempting to hide herself as her fingers dig at the rocks. Remembering the gun on the hood of the trunk, she jumps to grab it and falls back down, crouching at the front of the gate with the gun to her chest. She's afraid to run out in the open for fear her fate may end up like Levi and the others.

Shuddering, Séa remains almost as frozen as a chunk of ice until she decides to back into the street, keeping her eyes in front of her. When she gets about four feet away, another nail is shot, resulting in her falling prone to the ground with her chin buried in the dirt. She shifts back to the part of ground that's guarded by the front of the truck, struggling to keep quiet as she places one hand on her mouth while she holds the gun in her other.

The two-way road is empty with no cars coming either way as Séa waits anxiously for help, but nothing does for the short seconds she's lying on the ground.

She looks back at the nail jutting from Levi's head, takes a deep breath, and then, she makes a run for it down the barren road. She doesn't scream because there's no one to scream toward on the straight back road. Her breaths are short and shallow as she races down the middle of the road which is her only chance of escape, but when she looks back, the gate that the SUV blocked is now opening.

"Oh God!" She dashes to the side of the street to conceal herself in the thick rows of high grass, grass that reaches higher than her head. When she looks back, she sees the image of what she will forever know as the killer of the Doons staring down the empty street. Before turning away, she remembers her friends that she's leaving behind, all of them dead. Then she continues to tread through the high ground until she reaches safety far away.

Chapter Ten

"Ye though we walk through the valley of the shadow of death, we shall fear no evil, for You are with us Lord. It is Your rod and Your staff that comfort us."

The preacher leads the family and friends of all the bodies that didn't make it out of the Gates of Doons to the gravesites of each person that was discovered and taken to the morgue from where they lay deceased. The families all decide to bury them side by side, next to their late friend Justynn. In order from Justynn's grave going left to right is Pierre's coffin first, then Maria's, and continuing in the order of their deaths, Roscoe and Levi.

When the families gather around, news crews film from the sidewalk located a good distance away. Séa takes her seat in the center, staring without an expression at all the coffins before her. While she sits, the parents of each one killed take their seats, allowing their tears to flow and moans to grow louder and louder as a collective eulogy has been prepared for them all.

"Although these three young men and young lady left us behind in this old world," says the preacher who is fully robbed in white with a Bible in his hand that's lined with gold on all edges, "To be absent from the body is to be present with the LORD. Therefore, know in your hearts that the turmoil of life on this side can affect them no more. The sadness and the days of evil can't encamp around them...because God has made it so when He gives us rest. May they all rest with the LORD." His powerful voice mixed with the truth of God's Word moves the crowd to Amens. Some wail at this final word for the slain while others give glory to God that they don't have to suffer anymore, focusing on the knowledge that one day, they will all meet with them again. As far as Séa, she continues to sit with emptiness on her face all the way until they lower the coffins into the ground.

"The young men and woman that were murdered at the old Doons Mental Facility were buried today at Creations Cemetery. The four young adults just beginning their lives in college and working in their careers were assumed to have been attacked and killed by a man who was said to have been rehabilitated after years of psychological assessments. The name of the suspected killer is James Frazier, and he was first admitted into a psych ward at the age of seven when he stabbed four children to death while they played in their playroom. He was transferred from psych ward to psych ward until the Doons became his home over fifteen years ago, but when there was another slaughter, the mental facility shut down. James Frazier was nowhere to be found. If you have any information on this case, call the number at the bottom of the screen. There is a reward..."

Séa turns off the television in order to start the process of getting her life on another track. She's always been a person to progress from anything in her life to make it better, but this is her biggest challenge so far. As she goes into the kitchen to make a big glass of lemonade, she watches from the window as her mom and dad leave to go get something to eat. She turned down the ride with them, preferring to have them bring something back for her. From there, she closes the blinds and goes to slump down onto the floor of the living room. When she does, she drags the Holy Bible from the center table, the book she hasn't read for the longest time, and she cracks it open. She doesn't turn to Genesis, but to Psalm. Her dad, who just became a deacon in the church, would always read her something from the book of Psalm, Proverbs, Ephesians or Matthew before bedtime when she grew up, but she never decided to go there on her own. Tonight, as she glances up at the grandfather clock that is just striking eight, she will do just that – begin to read it on her very own from Psalm 91.

"He that dwelleth in the secret place of the most High shall abide under the shadow of the Almighty. I will say of the Lord, He is my refuge and my fortress: my God; in him will I trust. Surely he shall deliver thee from the snare of the fowler, and from the noisome pestilence. He shall cover thee with his feathers, and under his wings shalt thou trust: his truth shall be thy shield and buckler. Thou shalt not be afraid for the terror by night; nor for the arrow that flieth by day; Nor for the pestilence that walketh in darkness; nor for the destruction that wasteth at noonday. A thousand shall fall at thy side, and ten thousand at thy right hand; but it shall not come nigh thee. Only with thine eyes shalt thou behold and see the reward of the wicked. Because thou hast made the Lord, which is my refuge, even the most High, thy habitation; There shall no evil befall thee, neither shall any plague come nigh thy dwelling. For he shall give his angels charge over thee, to keep thee in all thy ways. They shall bear thee up in their hands, lest thou dash thy foot against a stone."

Séa then starts to weep heavily, the words of the scripture drowning in her tears but still just as powerful, yet for some reason, she can't grasp onto them. "I'm still so afraid, Father," she cries. "Please forgive me. I'm still so scared. I thought I was stronger than this." As she is speaking to God, trying to gain some insight on herself and what happened, she hears movement behind her. The movement is so quick and light that if it wasn't in between words during her prayer to God, she would have missed it. Quickly, she looks up and behind the kitchen bar counter, but sees nothing out of the ordinary. Then, she glances back at the Bible and gets up.

On her way to the garage to exercise, she grabs her headphones and iPod from the hallway. Making her way through the kitchen, she has a weird sense that someone is watching her, but she attributes her paranoia to the recent trauma of her life. Therefore, she continues into the garage which is converted into an exercise room.

As she mounts the exercise bike, she adjusts the settings and starts to pedal. She zones out when her favorite music hits her ears – pop. Of all the music in the world, she's always been drawn to pop with a hint of soul. Closing her eyes, she thinks of her deceased friends, the good times and bad. Mainly she thinks of Levi who gave his life to keep her alive, and tears begin to stream down her face. When she finally opens her eyes after about five minutes, her vision is all blurry. She reaches to turn the exercise bike off, but when she does, she knocks something off the top. Confused about what it is that she heard hit the floor, she wipes her eyes until she can see clearly and dismounts. When she looks down to the floor, there's a small rectangular shaped, black piece of hard plastic on the floor.

"Dang," she complains as she picks it up. "I knew this bike was a piece of garbage. I told them to buy the other one. This one's already coming apart."

She continues working out for about fifteen more minutes before she goes back inside the house. As she crosses the kitchen, she sits her iPod down to get a glass of water.

"Come on Séa. You can do this. Get back to your regular routine. It's not your fault." She places the glass underneath the automatic dispenser on the refrigerator and watches as the water pours inside the glass. "This is how you have to get your life again, Séa. Fill it back up," she continues, trying to encourage herself, and even imagining Levi telling her to keep going. When the glass is as full as it can get, she pours it down her throat, allowing some of the water to drizzle down the sides of her mouth.

She, then, walks back to her room where she ends up locked in a stare at the picture her and Levi took together. She opens a small drawer and gets more pictures of them all together, having fun, even when Justynn was alive. "I'll see you guys again. I promise." Lifting her hand to her mouth, she kisses it and then places her fingers onto the front of one of the group pictures. Afterwards, she takes off her shirt and shorts to jump in the shower, but she never makes it. She's stopped by what she sees laying on the floor before her at the base of the closed bathroom door.

Slowly, she walks over to it and kneels down, lifting it with her fingertips. It's her driver's license, the one that should have been confiscated along with the rest of the items left in the SUV. Her throat quakes, and her body begins to tremble until she drops her identification back on the floor, staring back at it as if her life is all a dream turning nightmare. Feeling like she's about to pass out, she grabs the sides of the bathroom doorway so she won't fall over, but then she spots the closest thing to her body – a desk lamp. With no hesitation, she snatches the lamp from the desk and spins around, shaking so badly that she almost loses her balance. The lamp was her only source of light in the bedroom, and now that she holds the lamp like a bat after ripping it from the plug, there's no longer any light in the room.

"Leave me alone," her voice quakes. No one is standing in front of her nor is anyone visibly standing anywhere in the bedroom. She turns quickly toward the bathroom and flicks the light switch to look at the pulled shower curtain, wondering if someone is standing behind it. She can't see any motion at all and becomes confused because she doesn't know where he is. The only thing she's sure of is that he's back, and he's come to kill her.

Slowly, she walks toward the bathroom's shower curtain, ready to pull it back and face the fight of her life. With each step, her stomach wants to give out. She wants run, but she can't because she doesn't know which direction to trust. Instead of walking any further toward the shower curtain, she backs out of the bathroom to take her stance between it and her queen sized bed. She stands there, shaking with the lamp inside her hand as she constantly looks both ways, waiting for a shadow to come by as the bathroom light shines into the room. Her leg hits the side of the bed while she backs into the wall, but then she stops breathing. Directly across from her is the closet. When she looks into the slits of the closet, the low moaning begins, and she knows that it's him. Like lightening, she leaps as fast as she can across her bed, however, she's too slow and the bed too wide for her to make it to the other side in one jump.

As she takes her first step from the bed, darting toward the door, she screams, "Help!" Her shrieks drill terror through the hallway walls until she feels a tight squeeze around the back of her neck, so tight to the point she thinks it will snap in two. She is then thrown to the other side of the room, her entire body banging against the wall and falling directly onto the floor. Her fear causes her to leap back up to try and run toward the window, but this time, she is grabbed by her ankles and slammed face first into the floor.

"Shhh!" He leans over the person whom he sees as just a rag doll and asks, "Remember me?"

Séa's mouth is busted open, and blood spills out as she cries, "Somebody!" She finds the strength to push her body up from the floor to crawl, but the psychopath kicks her back down. Then, he yanks her short, curly hair back, popping her neck. Séa can't even breathe anymore through her nose because it's bleeding profusely after the fall. She struggles to speak, "Please don't kill me. Just let me go." She doesn't get to see him face to face clearly until he stands her up and spins her around. As she spins like a paper doll in a music box, he hums a tune. When he finishes the song, he stops her to look into her eyes. Until this point, Séa has kept her eyes closed out of fear, but when he stops her, he orders her to open them.

"Peek," he orders, breathing heavily and thirsting for her response of obedience. When her eyes come fully open, he stares at her through the slits of his black mask and says, "A boo!" Then, through Séa's piercing screams for help, he head butts her viciously, and she passes out. Although she passes out, she remains upright as he allows her to hang from her hair that he's holding tightly in the air.

"Séa! Séa, baby girl, we're back, and we brought you some of your favorite!" her mom yells from the kitchen. "Joe, when you go back, will you check on her, and tell her to come up here with me while I fix up her plate. I want to try and get her to have a good night."

"Sure, baby." He gives his wife a small kiss on the lips, places his wallet on the counter and heads back down the hallway, expecting his daughter to be either soaking in her tub or sleeping. When he gets to her room, he calls her name but doesn't turn the light on, assuming she's in the bed. "Séa, sweetheart, we're home. You wanna come get something to eat?" When he gets no answer, he strolls into the room, empathetic for his daughter who has gone through so much pain and yet somehow survived, and sits on the side of the bed. "Hey?" He places his hands on the sheets and realizes that she isn't there. Then, he gets up and walks over to the light switch to turn it on. "Séa?"

Immediately, adrenaline rushes through is body when he sees a bloody floor and wall while the lamp her mother bought for her is thrown across the room. He rushes into the bathroom to find nothing, and then he speeds back down the hallway to get his wife.

"Symone, Séa isn't here! There's blood everywhere and the lamp..."

"Oh Jesus!" She drops the fresh food onto the floor and pushes past her husband to only find the same scene he described when she interrupted him. "Séa!" Symone hollers, but it doesn't help. Séa is nowhere to be found. She runs into Séa's bathroom and pulls back the shower curtain. Nothing. "Séa, baby! Joe, call the cops, call the cops!" she screams frantically, but he's already on the phone. As she searches the room, she spots the puddles of blood on the floor, and then she notices something that she'd walked right over when she went into the bathroom - Séa's driver's license. She checks the date issued, and then she falls against the wall, sliding down the side. Her husband notices that she has gone from bad to worse, and he runs to be by her side. When he gets there, he sees the reason why his wife slid down the wall.

"He's got her," he cries. "That killer...he's come back for my daughter!"

"Sir, please, calm down. We will get your daughter back if you just..." states the emergency personnel on the phone, but before she can finish her statement, the cell phone hits the floor.

Séa's head shakes back and forth, and as she regains consciousness while being dragged across the dirt between swarms of bushes and trees. She starts to kick, but no matter how forceful the kick, the powerful grip of the man dragging her by her ankles becomes just as strong, so she starts to scream.

"Help me! Somebody help me, please, help me. He's gonna kill me!" Each vine or branch she grabs easily snaps as the strength of the man she knows as the killer of the Doons forces her back to the gated building where her friend Maria died. She realizes rather quickly that the direction she is being dragged from isn't toward the front of the building, but rather from the back. She continues to fight to free herself, but when she reaches the building's gates, her head slams against the concrete that lines the tall grass.

She continues to beg and plead with him, but her begging falls on deaf ears as he pulls her legs up higher toward his chest. He grabs a long blade, releases of one of her ankles, and to the other, he slices through her Achilles tendon. Séa screams horribly, the most terrifyingly painful scream ever imagined, and then he drops her leg. Pain rips through Séa's foot and leg as she makes the valiant effort to get away on one leg, but collapses when the killer leans over, grabs the other leg and slices that Achilles tendon as well. Her screams are no more than a whisper because no matter how hard she cries, no one hears her.

With a tightly woven rope, he begins to tie her legs together after crossing them at the ankles he just ripped to shreds. All the fight in Séa is gone as she lies there on the cement only watching the tears bubble up in her eyes. From there, he ties her wrists together followed by tying them to her body tightly so that she can't even wiggle her arms. Finally, when she is bound, he lifts her into his arms. Séa panics once again although she can't give much a fight at all. She bucks her body as hard as she can while shouting for anyone, including her mom and dad. She does this continuously until the killer finally speaks.

"I never lose." Then, he steps atop a large stone, and with her secured in his arms, he holds her further up and forcefully shoves her down atop the sharp, wrought iron spearheads of the gate that line the inner perimeter of where she once escaped – the Doons. The spearheads hold her up as she struggles to breathe, but during her struggle, he shoves her further downward, causing the spearheads to sink deeper into her body. Blood starts to drain from her mouth until she takes her last breath, meeting her fate while she loses sight of the night sky.

**

"It was just last week that four young adults were brutally murdered at the old Doons facility and were even buried yesterday. Today, unfortunately, there is more news. A horrible turn of events came to the lone survivor of the terrible ordeal. Séa Moody, the last female survivor, was killed last night, and according to a leaked police report, she was taken back to the site of the original murders, the same exact spot where her friends were left dead. According to the leaked police record, I'm sorry," reports the news anchor, "but this is very graphic, therefore, we won't describe the scene. However, there is little doubt anymore that the killer is in fact that same person who massacred several children a long time ago. His name he wrote in the cement with Séa Moody's blood - James Frazier."

The killer of the Doons is still on the loose.

The End

More Akirim Press Books

Books by Mirika Mayo Cornelius

Secret

Colored Lily: Poppa Took My Innocence

Paton

Ain't Quite What I Thought!

Ain't Quite What I Thought! 2

Inside the Gates of Doons

Sunny Sides of My Shade

Murders at Gabriel's Trails: The Complete 5 Part Series plus bonus Sins of Bain

Books by Rod Cornelius

Diggin' Gold

The Trusted

Single Again

Ghetto Eyes

The Best Kept Secrets

Ugly

Books by Cyan Deane

Dead Man's Mayhem

Execution's Karma

Preview Murders at Gabriel's Trials: The Complete 5 Part Series plus bonus Sins of Bain by Mirika Mayo Cornelius

Alexis spots Bain walking casually down the trail with his confident swag and cell phone to his ear. Whoever he was talking to, Alexis doesn't care. For the most part, she's just ecstatic to see that he is coming up the trail to meet her like her knight in shining armor. She trusts him so much until she feels like absolutely nothing can hurt her in the world, including in Gabriel's Trails. Besides that, Bain is well known for his handsomely strong stature and no hesitations when it comes to taking care of any trouble that comes his way. He's never killed anyone, however, but after he's finished dealing with anyone who crosses him, the word is that the victim of his anger wishes Bain had taken his life.

Bain is about six feet two in height, medium build but built into a brown skinned body that any woman would love, including young girl. He has a youthfulness about him that appeals to all the women because although he is all about no nonsense when it comes to what belongs to him, he's also tender and respectful and can make any woman blush, let alone a teenager. It is Alexis that has his heart though, and most ladies know this.

He's finally within arms' reach of Alexis and pauses before reaching out to embrace her. "Why did you walk this far up, Lex? You know I don't let you walk this far up the trail..."

"I'm a big girl, babe," she responds, tip toeing to plant him a kiss on the lips while he stands there and takes it all in, rubbing the small of her back like he wants to undress her on the spot. The trail is lined by trees on both sides, and as Bain pulls back from the kiss, he gently turns her backwards so that she can see why coming this far into Gabriel's Trails is dangerous.

"Do you see the main road anymore, Lex?"

"No, Bain," she drags.

"Nothing but a trail that ends, curving back into where you came from. Nobody can see you anymore, Lex. At that point," he explains, pointing to a boulder that's painted red on the side of the trail, "Coming in here beyond that rock this far up means that you're on your own." He turns her back around so that he can look her in the eyes. "I don't ever want you to be on your own, Lex."

"Like I said, I got me."

Preview SECRET by Mirika Mayo Cornelius

"I told you your aunt is resting, didn't I?"

I reach my leg back and kick him in his mouth. He yanks his head back and stares at me like he's gonna kill me, so I kick him again with both of my legs swinging like a wild bat. He jumps on top of me holding my right leg with his hand and ducking away from my other leg while its kicking. He starts to unbuckle his pants with his other hand.

"Yeah, it's present time now. You done asked for it. I heard about your momma. A nice piece of work there."

He rips off my pajamas after he gets his pants down. My heart fills up with scary feelings when I just now figure out why my Aunt May said what she told me all the time. Where's Aunt Janie?

"Aunt Janie! Your friend is in my room! He's not supposed to be in here, Aunt Janie!" I yell the loudest I can yell.

Sam reaches back with his right hand and hits me on the side of my stomach. I curl up in a ball.

"Guess what, Secret. She ain't coming so ain't no use in you calling for her. You act like I'm about to hurt you. I wouldn't have hit you like that if you didn't try to wake up your aunt, so I'm sorry. Now hold still."

He feels up my back with his naked hand. My stomach is aching. He keeps acting like he ain't gonna do nothing to me, but this don't feel right. I keep thinking about Aunt May while his hand is going up my leg. I feel something wet on my leg, too. I yank away, but he jerks me in front of him. Jesus, please, help me, Lord. Tears are falling every which way down my face, but then I see it. I fell asleep with my pencil beside me in my bed. It's halfway covered up with my sheets.

"Touch it."

I look back at him, and he closes his eyes.

"Look down and touch it."

That's when I look down and see what he's talking about. I panic.

"Get off of me! No! I'm not touching that thing-ever! What is that? Aunt Janie, please!" I reach for the pencil real fast, but I don't know what to do with it yet. My hand grips the pencil like somebody else got it for me. My other hand grabs that long, ugly thing, and my hand, with the pencil in it, reaches all the way back and stabs that big, ugly thing right in the center.

He lets out the loudest holler I ever heard from a man in my life, and his eyes fly open. I jump up off the bed, and run towards the other end of my room. I look back at his ugly thing and see that the pencil is still stuck in there while he's tumbling around on the floor. His hands are around it, but he ain't pulling it out. It's hurtin' him so bad that I pick up my lamp so that I can aim for his head so I can bang some more pain into him. He justa hollering. Betcha he won't come in my room no more.

Preview Diggin' Gold by Rod Cornelius

She wanted him just as bad as he wanted her, but just not bad enough to get it on in the car. She also realized that another round with Trent meant another day of lying to Jimmy, but what he doesn't know wouldn't hurt him, she thought. Besides, she was trying to come up and Jimmy's stock was falling fast. Trent had tangible assets, and she was almost ready to go all in.

"I told you earlier that I had a lack of patience for you. Now how about let's get up out of this ride and take a no-holds barred tour of my humble abode. There won't be a piece of furniture off limits. I promise," he said as he continued feasting on her neck.

She observed his house again, "I don't know if you got a back strong enough for the kind of tour that you're talking about. Your place looks like it has a lot of ground to cover. It could take the whole night to get it all."

He pulled up and backed away from her. "There's only one way to find out."

"Then why are we still in your Jag?"

He backed away further with a smile as she smiled right back at him. "Baby, it ain't nothing but a word."

"Then what are you waiting on?"

"Shiiiiiit!" he said. She finally told him what his ears had been waiting all night to hear. The green light was lit. He knew he could have pretty much any woman he set his sights on but Kizzy carried an extra spiff. Not only was she sexy and a freak in between the sheets, but she was Jimmy's lady. She was the last thing he could take from Jimmy and that was worth more than its weight in gold.

He quickly hopped out of the automobile and danced around the vehicle to open her door. He grabbed her hand to assist her on her exodus. He shut the door, not releasing her hand as they made their way to his front door.

As she stood behind him, she looked up and admired the huge brick home. She had never been in a house as big as his, and she couldn't wait to serenade it with him. "This really is a nice place, Trent. I could see you making me some pancakes in bed here," she joked.

"Oh we 'bout to make something, but it's not going to pancakes, that's for sure." He pulled her into the dark house and slammed the door shut. Then he pulled her into him and gave her a passionate kiss.

"So I guess you mean business," she said as she pulled away from his lips and rested her arms around his neck.

"Do I?" he smiled. He placed both hands on her rump and gripped it tightly, pulling her up off of the floor as she wrapped her legs around his waist. As his tongue ran its slow, slippery course up and down her neck, he walked her through the dark living space and carried her to the leather couch. He laid her down and his tongue twirled around her bosom as his hands made their way down her legs as he began to inch her dress upwards.

Preview Dead Man's Mayhem by Cyan Deane

What the hell was that? If they don't get their little southern asses out of my viewing! Rest in peace? Mary made my life a living, breathing, stinking hell, and she has her sweaty panties coming in here trying to start some real shit while I'm still trying to wake myself up from this doomsday nightmare.

Mary – she's the lady that built the straw house that I wanted to crap on each and everyday to make that thing fall down right on top of her ass. When I would walk into her bar, for some reason or another, she would always be there. What owner is always at their establishment? That's the purpose of hiring people to work for you while you sit your ass at home and play golf in the middle of lunch time traffic so everyone can see what a grand life you have. She would make her baggy eyeballs twitch at me, and she's only forty one years old, looking and sounding like a grandma of eight hell raisers.

Truth be told, Mary would constantly talk shit, but it was shit that I could never hear. Call me paranoid, but she was ten words from getting popped in her mouth the day I supposedly went cold. I still don't even know who knocked me over my damn head in her nasty ass bar, but I swear it was probably her ass that set me up. She hated me, and I could tell. Her raggedy bar wasn't even that good for anything, but I was determined to go inside each and every week to make her life-long dream of store ownership reek of irritation with my presence.

I'd come to find out that I dated Mary's second cousin, Barbara Sue, back in the day for like three minutes tops, and Barbara Sue had gone and told her whole felon ass family that I was the one who broke her heart into pieces. First off, what they didn't know was that I would have never dated anyone seriously named Barbara Sue. Let's get that out there right now. Secondly, all I did was kiss her after talking on the phone with her for about one week.

When I met up with her, Barbara Sue wasn't really my type, but hell, the date was still on. We went to see a movie, parked it at the park, kissed and I took her snaggle toothed mouth home. It's true I never called again, but it was a damn shame how she ran my name in the mud about it.

Preview Single Again by Rod Cornelius

"Hey, do you have a name?" She didn't answer. She blatantly ignored me, just like she did when I first approached her in the club. Now see, it's things like that, that makes a man think with his brain and not his jimmy all of the time. But then I took another glance at her body and quickly realized how much more powerful a man's jimmy is than his brain. As a matter of fact, it is his brain. Besides, this chick was a perfect ten. A ten, then some. And those are just too hard to come by at times.

Her directions led me straight to a two-story brick house smack-dab in the middle of Brenton Avenue. "Keys," she chillingly requested. A brief thought of being stranded in the middle of nowhere swiftly raced through my mind. I gave her the keys. "Come on," she said. Thank you, Jesus. I couldn't bare the thought of walking all the way back to that club and trying to quickly compose a lie to Rex as to why I was perspiring so badly.

I jumped out of the car and shadowed her tracks like a starving dog sniffing for a meaty bone. She opened the door to the house and flicked on the lights beside the entrance. As I stepped into her crib, I began to instantly think that this experience had to be some kind of cruel joke sponsored by my subconscious and somehow, I was sleeping and couldn't wake up. And the way it was beginning to feel, this was gonna be a wet one.

She glanced back at me, "Close the door." I shut the door and followed her up the stairs. The house really didn't have much in it. In fact, it looked unlived in altogether. The walls were neatly entangled with an assortment of oil paintings but not much furniture consumed the home. Nonetheless, my primary concern rested on just one piece of furniture in particular▮▮▮the bed!

We walked into what had to have been the master bedroom. It was humongous. An exquisite Persian rug laced the floor. There was a huge floor-length window open, and the nightly breeze blew her finely-silk draperies into the room. Most significantly of all, she had this massive king-sized bed in the center of the room.

I looked around, not trying to seem overly-amazed. "So this is yours?"

"Nope!" she said as she walked alongside her bed, slowly sliding her fingers across the satin sheets.

Damn! I knew she had to have a man, somewhere.

"Well, it is for now. My agency is leasing this place for me until I find some place to live down here," she said.

"Oh," I said relieved that there was no sign of any manly presence in her life so far. "All this for you, huh?"

She grinned. "Yeap."

I walked over to the window and gazed down at the dimly lit street. I didn't want to seem too anxious for what she had to offer. "Nice view."

"I'll say," she replied.

I could almost feel her eyes cutting through my back. I turned around, thinking maybe I could slip a little bit of my own arrogance in there. "I was referring to the street."

"I was, too. What else would I be referring to?"

Ooh, low blow, and can't say that I didn't deserve it. As she took a seat on the bed, I just stared at her, not having a clue to where things were headed. But if I knew anything, I definitely had to have them go the direction I wanted them to.

"So," I took a deep breath. "Why did you bring me here?"

"Why did you come?" she quickly combated.

"What? You grabbed my hand and led the way."

"You're a grown man. I'm quite sure you could've stopped me."